MW01077020

Welcome to Land of Fright™

Land of Fright™ is a world of spine-tingling short horror stories filled with the strange, the eerie, and the weird. The **Land of Fright™** series encompasses the vast expanse of time and space. You will visit the world of the Past in Ancient Rome, Medieval England, the old West, World War II, and other eras yet to be explored. You will find many tales that exist right here in the Present, tales filled with modern lives that have taken a turn down a darker path. You will travel into the Future to tour strange new worlds and interact with alien societies, or to just take a disturbing peek at what tomorrow may bring.

Each **Land of Fright™** story exists in its own territory (which we like to call a **terrorstory**.) These terrorstories can be visited in any order you choose. Some of the story realms you visit will intrigue you. Some of them may unsettle you. Some of them may even titillate and amuse you. We hope many of them will give you delicious chills along your journey. And there are many new uncharted realms yet to be mapped, so keep checking back for new discoveries.

First, we need to check your ID. **Land of Fright™** is intended for mature audiences. You will experience adult language, graphic violence, and some explicit sex. Ready to enter? Good. We'll take that ticket now. **Land of Fright™** awaits. You can pass through the dark gates and—Step Into Fear!

Readers Love Land of Fright™!

"This is the first story I've read by this author and it blew me away! A gripping tale that kept me wondering until the end. Images from this will, I fear, haunt me at unexpected moments for many months to come. Readers, be warned! :)" – Amazon review for **Dung Beetles (Land of Fright™ #27 - in Collection III)**

"Some truly original stories. At last, a great collection of unique and different stories. Whilst this is billed as horror, the author managed to steer away from senseless violence and gratuitous gore and instead with artful story telling inspires you to use your own imagination. A great collection. Already looking for other collections… especially loved Kill the Queen (God Save the Queen)." – Amazon UK review for **Land of Fright™ Collection I**

"This was a great story. Even though it was short I still connected with the main character and was rooting for her. Once I read the twist I cheered her on. This was an enjoyable short story." – Amazon review for **Snowflakes (Land of Fright™ #3 – in Collection I)**

"Four stars. Real strange story." – Amazon UK review for **Hitler's Graveyard (Land of Fright™ #25 – in Collection III)**

"Loved the twist. A good short story with a hilarious twist. Great lunch time read." – Amazon review for **Trophy Wives (Land of Fright™ #5 – in Collection I)**

"…a good read. Well-written and entertaining." – Amazon review for **Special Announcement (Land of Fright™ #11 – in Collection II)**

"Another great story; I've become a fan of Mr. O'Donnell. Please keep them coming…" – Amazon review for **Sands of the Colosseum (Land of Fright™ #18 – in Collection II)**

"Perfect bite size weirdness. Land of Fright does it again with this Zone like short that has two creative plot twists that really caught me off guard. I know comparing this type of work to the Twilight Zone is overdone but it really is a high compliment that denotes original, well conceived and delightfully weird short fiction. Recommended." – Amazon review for **Flipbook (Land of Fright™ #19 – in Collection II)**

"An enjoyable story; refreshingly told from the point of view of the cat…definitely good suspense." – Amazon review for Pharaoh's **Cat (Land of Fright™ #30 – in Collection III)**

"An enjoyable story, as always. Well-written and keeps you wondering…." – Amazon review for **The Tinies (Land of Fright™ #28 – in Collection III)**

"This short has a cool premise and was very effective at quickly transporting me to the sands of the coliseum in ancient Rome. The images of dead and dying gladiators are detailed and vivid. There is a malevolent force that very much likes its job and is not about to give it up, ever. Recommended." – Amazon review for **Hammer of Charon (Land of Fright™ #29 – in Collection III)**

"The thing I like about the Land of Fright series of short stories is that they are so diverse yet share a common weird, unusual and original vibe. From horror to science fiction they are all powerful despite of their brevity. Another great addition to the Land of Fright festival of the odd." - Amazon review for **Snowflakes (Land of Fright™ #3 – in Collection I)**

"I like the idea of a malevolent dimension that finds a way to reach into our world… this was an entertaining read and can be read at lunch or as a palate cleanser between longer stories." – Amazon review for **Sparklers (Land of Fright™ #15 – in Collection II)**

"Pool of light was such a great story. It gave you just enough information to let your mind take over and it was a story you could read on your break. I liked how it wasn't a typical horror story. Would highly recommend." – Amazon review for **Pool of Light (Land of Fright™ #13 – in Collection II)**

"I enjoyed this quite a bit, but then I enjoy anything set in Pompeii. A horror story is a first, though, and well done. I'm become a fan of the author and so far have enjoyed several of his stories." – Amazon review for **Ghosts of Pompeii (Land of Fright™ #14 – in Collection II)**

"Fantastic science fiction short that has a surprising plot twist, great aliens, cool future tech and occurs in a remote lived-in future mining colony on a distant planet. This short hit all the marks I look for in science fiction stories. The alien creatures are truly alien and attack with a mindless ruthlessness. The desperate colonists defend themselves in a uniquely futuristic way. This work nails the art of the short story. Recommended." – Amazon review for **Out of Ink (Land of Fright™ #26 – in Collection III)**

"A harried corporate drone is presented with a bizarre choice when he stumbles onto the beginning of a unbelievable world changing event occurring in a hidden basement floor of his corporate office. This tale had me wondering, what would I do? This short fits right in with the theme of the entertaining and delightfully offbeat Land of Fright series: weird, unexpected, powerful and surreal short fiction. Recommended."- Amazon reviews for **The Tinies (Land of Fright™ #28 – in Collection III)**

Land of Fright™

Collection II

JACK O'DONNELL

All Land of Fright™ Stories
Copyright © 2014-2017 Jack O'Donnell

Land of Fright™ - Collection II
Copyright © 2015 Jack O'Donnell

All rights reserved. No portion of this work may be reproduced or transmitted, in any form by any means, without the express written permission of the author.

Published by ODONNELL BOOKS

All persons and events in these stories are fictitious. The Land of Fright™ doesn't exist. Or does it?

Some images from Deposit Photos, Dreamstime, Wikimedia Commons. Used under their respective licenses. Other images from the author's own collection.

ISBN-10: 1940118093
ISBN-13: 978-1-940118-09-3

Visit www.landoffright.com

DEDICATION

To all the comic book artists and writers who gave me a happy childhood filled with great stories and grand adventures. Not sure how I turned out this way, but it wasn't your fault...

LAND OF FRIGHT™
COLLECTION II
CONTENTS

TERRORSTORY #11
SPECIAL ANNOUNCEMENT

Bears Beat Packers 36-30 in Overtime Thriller!

The sign blinked the news repeatedly half a dozen times. *Go Bears*, Charles Montague thought and smiled. He was a balding man in his late forties, thin wire-rimmed glasses adorning his face. He glanced up to see the stoplight was still red. He looked back at the electronic sign on the other side of the intersection. It was a new sign the village had erected only a few days ago. The next message flashed across the screen, announcing a pancake breakfast at the local American Legion on Saturday morning. *I need to hit that*, Charles thought. *Nothing like a good short stack with maple syrup and melted butter on a Saturday morning.*

Today was turning out to be a good day. He had finally broken off his affair with Melody. It was over. For real this time. They had to stop before his wife found out. Melody had not taken it well, but he was pretty certain she got the message when he called her a dumb bitch. It was stupid to have ever started anything with her. Melody and his wife Vivian both worked in the village hall. In the same damn building, for crying out loud. Not even thirty feet away from each other. The affair was way too dangerous to continue.

Something nagged at Charles about the Bears announcement, but his thoughts kept turning to Melody. That luscious blonde hair, that little pert nose, those sensual lips. Their illicit affair had been triggered by just a simple offer of coffee. He had been standing in the outer office area of the village hall, waiting for Vivian to finish her meeting, minding his own business, when Melody offered to get him a cup of coffee. He didn't usually go to the village hall much, but Vivian's Dart was in the shop getting new belts, so he had to pick his wife up after work. "Sure," he had said to Melody's offer with a shrug.

Melody climbed out from behind her desk and he couldn't help but notice the tight body she had under her tight skirt. She had an incredibly shapely ass. And she knew how to draw attention to it. She sashayed over to the coffee machine with a sublime swish of her hips and poured him a cup. Then she asked him if he'd like some cream and sugar. And the way it came out of her mouth sounded like she asked him if he wanted to fuck her hard in the mouth or take her from behind. Charles still remembered how hard he got just looking and listening to Melody. They had talked several times before at various events and he had enjoyed her company, but this took their communication to a whole new level.

Then came some flirty casual touches. Brief touches of fingers. Bodies brushing against each other as they moved past each other. He made up some problems with his village licensing so they would have a cover for their rendezvous. They met a few times for secret lunches. Then they fucked. Right on Melody's desktop after hours. *God damn, that was hot.* His cock twitched in his pants. Melody had the keys to close up the village hall, so it was easy for them to meet whenever they wanted to late at night. His wife Vivian was an early to bed early to rise kind of woman, so it was pretty easy to slip out at night and slip it into Melody.

Charles later found out he was just a rebound from a bad relationship Melody had just gone through, but he didn't care. She was hot. The sex was hot. He knew he would miss her. She gave the best blow jobs ever, but he knew he had to stop. His cock twitched again, the pulsing stronger now. *Jesus, stop. It's done. It's over. You can't go crawling back to her. You're the one who ended it.* She was becoming way too possessive, way too demanding of his time. Despite his mental protests, his cock stiffened.

Charles heard a horn honk loudly behind him. He looked up to see the light had turned green; he stepped on the accelerator. Something still nagged at him about the Bears announcement, but the feeling vanished as a black van nearly cut him off. He shouted a dozen profanities at the damned idiot and the message on the village sign board was forgotten.

At least for the moment.

━━━━◆━━━━

Charles leaned forward on the couch, intently watching the action unfold on his big screen TV, the potato chips and the open beer on the table next to him temporarily forgotten. *What a game!* The Packers had tied the game with a last second field goal, sending it into overtime. It was tied thirty to thirty and the Bears were driving down the field.

Bears Beat Packers 36-30 in Overtime Thriller.

The memory of the sign flashed into his head. *Wait a minute,* he thought. *The game hadn't even been played yet, so how could they have announced the score? What the hell? That's crazy.* "I know what the final score is," Charles said.

Vivian sat on the couch nearby, doing some of their bills. His wife was a petite woman with short curly brown hair. She had a fleece blanket draped over her lap. She glanced up at him. "What?"

He pointed to the TV. "I know what the score is going to be."

Vivian looked at him with a blank face. She wasn't much of a football fan.

"It's going to be thirty-six to thirty. Bears win."

Vivian wasn't impressed by his prediction. "Okay." She returned her attention to the stack of bills next to her.

Charles stared with rapt fascination at the game being played live on his television.

The Bears won on a forty-two yard touchdown pass, caught off a defender's bobbled interception attempt. The Bears did beat the Packers. The score was thirty-six to thirty. And it *was* an overtime thriller.

That's not possible, Charles thought. *That is just not*

6

freakin' possible. How could that sign have flashed the final score before the game had been played? The question played itself over and over again in his mind. *Did I just imagine that message? No, I saw it. I saw that announcement clear as day on that sign.*

Charles had a restless sleep that night. He knew who was in charge of putting the village messages on that electronic sign. He knew her very well. *How did she know what the score was going to be?* He knew Melody was into fortune telling and astrology and all that hoodoo voodoo kind of shit. *Did she see it in the cards?* He mentally scoffed. *Really? Maybe she saw it in the stars, you fucking idiot. Now she's a seer with psychic powers? She just made a damn lucky guess.*

He dreamed of Melody's mouth.

Charles was afraid to look at the sign, but its silent siren call was too strong to overcome. He looked.

Shred Day 9AM-Noon at the Village Hall. The message scrolled off the screen. Another message appeared. **Home Business Expo - High School Gym 3-8PM.**

He breathed a sigh of relief. They were simple announcements that made sense. He did have some shredding he needed to do. It would be a great excuse to see Melody again. *No, you damn fool. It's way too early to see her again. You know what will happen. Stay away from her. Let it be. It's only a few stacks of papers. It won't take long to shred them.* His cock stirred.

A horn honked behind him. Charles looked up to see the light was green. He hit the accelerator and moved through the intersection, consciously avoiding looking anywhere near the sign as he drove past it.

He drove to his office on Burroughs Avenue and started his day. He had half a dozen cases waiting for him. He was the local director of the National Advertising Division of the Great Lakes Chamber of Commerce, in charge of investigating false advertising claims made by businesses in his region. He loved taking down charlatans and quacks and blatant lying scumbags. There was nothing worse than being burned by some bullshit deception that was just outright fraud. He hated that feeling himself and did his best to prevent others from experiencing it. Deceptive advertising was just plain evil and the world was better off without it. Somebody had to watch out for the little people.

Charles looked over at the two bins full of loose paper sitting on the floor near his desk. He needed to shred those. He frowned. He needed to stop thinking of Melody's mouth.

⋙⋘

Burroughs Avenue Closed. Take Alternate Route.

Charles read the flashing message again. He frowned. The last few days had been very uneventful. The messages on the sign had been typical, announcing upcoming events like Play Day in the Park, new library hours, and other such normal things. But this message felt different to him. The building he had just purchased for his new office a few months ago was on Burroughs Avenue. There was no alternative route; it was a cul-de-sac with only one way in and one way out.

The light turned green and he drove on.

Burroughs Avenue was still open when he reached it. He frowned. Maybe they had been doing some construction work earlier. He mentally shrugged. Whatever. It was still open and accessible.

Charles put in a solid fours of work and then went out for lunch. For a brief moment, he thought he saw Melody sitting in a parked car near his office as he drove by. *Maybe I should call her?* His cock twitched. But when he looked back the woman was gone.

The black smoke spiraling up into the sky had been his first clue that something was wrong. The two police cars blocking the entrance to Burroughs Avenue was the second clue. The red fire truck parked near his new office was definitely the third and final clue.

The fire licking the sky where his office used to be completed the puzzle. The building was already completely obliterated by the flames. The sides were blackened with soot. The roof had already collapsed. Dozens of firefighters worked frantically about the scene, some pulling hoses, some already spraying water onto the blaze.

Charles pulled his car over to the side of the road and stepped out, bracing his arm on the open driver's side door. He looked up at the flames and just watched them burn his office.

A police officer came over to him. "Sorry, the road's closed for now."

"That's my office," Charles said.

The police officer looked at the decimated building, then back at Charles. "Not anymore."

Charles just looked at the officer mutely. He sat back down in the car. He looked down at his hands as they lay curled in his lap. His fingers trembled.

⧫≈⟨◉⟩≈⧫

Charles drove to the village hall to tell Vivian the bad news. He could have just called her or texted her, but he didn't. He wasn't much of a cell phone user. He had one in his pocket, but hardly ever turned the damned thing on. He didn't like to feel so connected to everything and everyone. The cell phone made him feel tethered to the world. Besides, maybe Melody would be there. Maybe she would feel sorry for him. Maybe she would give him a sympathetic hug. And then...

Vivian was out when he arrived at the village hall, visiting some local businesses. The receptionist thought she was going to be back soon, but she wasn't sure. She let him in to Vivian's outer office to wait.

Melody sat at her desk just outside the mayor's office door. She did not greet him when he entered the room, or even look up at him, so he kept silent. She looked amazing. She had curled her hair so it framed her face quite elegantly. She had her tortoise shell glasses on instead of her contacts. He didn't know why, but the sight of Melody in glasses always gave him a raging hard on. Just as it did now.

He moved over to a nearby chair and sat. He glanced at the ragtag pile of magazines on the coffee table in front of him, but nothing grabbed his attention. *What the hell am I going to do about a new office? Son of a bitch.* It was too much to think about. Too overwhelming right now.

Charles cast furtive glances at Melody, but he never caught her looking at him. She kept herself busy on her computer, clacking at the keyboard. He could hear her fingernails hitting the keys in a steady rhythm, but the silence between them had a thickness to it. It was an unpleasant feeling that poked and pinched and pulled at him. *I should never have called her a dumb bitch*, he thought.

He could smell the subtle hint of her perfume. *I used to bury my face in that smell*, he remembered. *And then I used to bury my face between her legs.* Melody had a sweet taste to her. Not like the sour pungent taste Vivian had. Charles crossed his legs, trying to squeeze the hardness out of his cock.

He got tired of waiting after twenty minutes. "Hey, Melody," he finally said to crack the wall of silence that separated them. "How are you?"

Melody stopped typing. She held her fingers stock still above the keyboard for a long moment. She glanced down to her right but he couldn't see what she was looking at because of the low wall of her cubicle. She reached over and grabbed something, then raised it up slowly to show him. It was a tarot card. A tarot card depicting a skeleton wrapped in a black robe clutching a sickle. The tarot card of Death.

It was the most chilling thing he had ever seen in his life. He thought about laughing, but the moment wasn't funny. It wasn't funny at all. And then she raised her face to look at him and the dark intent in her eyes sent a cold flood of chills racing through his entire body. It was a look of malevolent evil. His erection drained and his penis turtled into a shriveled lump the size of a thimble. He looked away and quickly rose out of his chair.

"Have a nice life," Melody said as he headed out the door.

⟢⟣⟐⟢⟣

Charles stared at the sign in utter disbelief. *What the fuck kind of sick joke is that?* Melody had gone too far. He glanced around at the other drivers near him. They seemed oblivious to the announcement on the sign. A young girl in the car next to him was busy texting on her phone. An elderly man to his right was staring intently straight ahead, his withered hands gripping the steering wheel tightly. Charles looked up again at the message on the sign.

His thoughts raced and he had a hard time focusing them. His office just burned down and now this. *Jesus, my office burned down! How the fuck did that happen?* The enormity of it finally hit him. *I haven't backed up the server in months! Son of a fucking bitch. I lost a shitload of data. Fuck, fuck, fuck!* He slammed his palms against the steering wheel.

His heart pounded in his chest, in his ears. He could feel sweat lining his entire body. His hands shook despite the ferocious grip he had on the steering wheel; his knuckles turned bone white. He glanced up at the red light. *Come on, you fuck! Change!* The light stayed a deep red.

Charles looked back at the sign. The message did not scroll, or blink, or flash. It remained bright and visible on the screen, the words in red luminescent letters on the black background. He shifted in the driver's seat, squirming uselessly for some avenue of escape when there was none.

He looked back up at the stoplight. Red. *Fuck!* He pounded the steering wheel. "Fucking change!" The light remained red. He grabbed the steering wheel and shook it violently. His breathing was hot and ragged. Sweat dripped into his right eye and he swiped it away angrily with the back of his hand, dislodging his glasses for a moment to get at the stinging sweat.

He looked up at the message and felt his heart tighten in his chest. *I can't wait. I can't wait. I have to get home.* Charles slammed down on the accelerator and pulled out into the intersection.

Just then, another vehicle came racing into the intersection from his right. His car slammed into the other car hard, crashing square into the driver's side door. Metal crunched. Glass shattered. Two shotgun-loud blasts rang in Charles's ears as his airbag deployed, inflating straight at him, blinding him to everything around him. The rough nylon fabric scratched at his face and neck. The acrid smell of gunpowder coming from the deployed airbag assailed his nose.

And then everything was still for a moment. Charles heard other car doors slam, voices in the distance. The voices drew closer. "Jesus, look at her," a voice said.

Charles pushed the deflating airbag out of the way. Even through the hazy cloud of smoke that filled his car, the sign immediately demanded his attention. Somehow his glasses were still in place on his face. One of the rims on his glasses was bent, and his left lens had a spiderweb of cracks running through it, but he could still see out of them. He stared at the message he had been reading over and over again for the last minute.

Mayor Vivian Montague Dead at 42.

Charles looked at the car he had just collided with.

He recognized it. It was their Dart. It was his wife's car. A mangled female body lay halfway out the open door. Blood pooled on the road beneath the body. Her face was coated in blood, so much that she was barely recognizable. But he recognized her. He recognized Vivian's face. Her eyes were open and they did not blink.

"She's dead," a voice said.

Charles heard the proclamation loud and clear. He just killed the mayor. His wife was dead. Vivian was dead.

The sign changed, the new message flashing bright red on the black background, demanding attention. He looked away from the destruction and up at the sign.

Charles Montague Committed to the Lancaster Rehabilitation Facility.

I'm going to the nuthouse, he thought as he read the special announcement through his mangled and cracked glasses. *The sign doesn't lie. I'm going to the nuthouse.* Charles Montague started to laugh and he couldn't stop scratching the itching red rash that covered his face and neck.

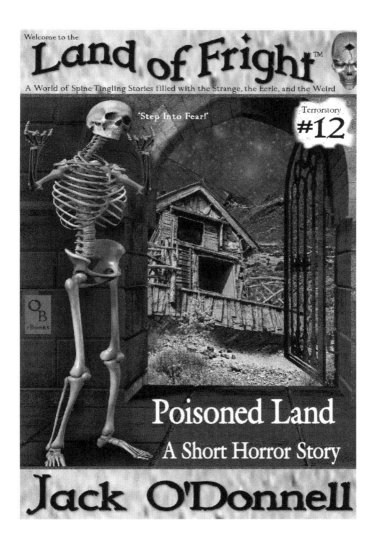

TERRORSTORY #12
POISONED LAND

"You can't go out there! The land is poisoned!"

Toby Draper grabbed Jim's upper arm, tugging him back onto the platform. Toby had a lean face with high cheekbones. His blond hair was a little wild and unruly with the hint of natural curls trying to take over from the straight haircut he sported.

Jim Cunningham worked at easing Toby's grip from his arm, prying at his fingers. "I'm sick of being trapped," he said. Jim was a bit on the pudgy side and his face showed it. His black hair was cut short, making his face seem even rounder.

"Are you out of your mind?" Toby asked. He

released his hold on Jim's arm. "You going stir crazy?" He reached out and put the back of his hand against Jim's forehead. "You got a touch of fever?"

Jim slapped his hand away.

Toby slowly lowered his hand. He looked at Jim for a moment, then sat in one of the wooden chairs that was positioned nearby.

Jim took the chair beside Toby, lowering his portly body into the seat. He exhaled heavily. "I just wanted to test it."

"Test it? With bare feet?" Toby shook his head. "Not a good idea. That poison will seep right into your feet and go straight for your heart. You'd take two steps and keel over dead."

"Maybe it's desilated."

"Desilated?"

Jim nodded. "You know, like dissolved. Desilated."

Toby laughed. "You mean dissipated." He shook his head. "No, it doesn't *desilate* and it doesn't dissipate either. It stays in the ground. You can't see it, but it's there. Trust me, it's there. The whole damn area all around us is poisoned. We are trapped."

They sat in silence for a long moment. The sun blazed high and hot in the afternoon sky.

"So how do we get past it?" Jim asked.

Toby shook his head. "There is no way to get past it," he said.

Jim thought about that for a moment. "Poisons usually have antidotes, right? Then we need to find the antidote."

Toby nodded with a few fast jerks of his head up and down. "Good thinking." But then his enthusiasm faded as quickly as it had risen. A frown tugged his lips down.

"What?" Jim asked.

"Antidote is a good idea, but look." Toby waved his arm out in front of him, motioning to the expanse beyond the platform they were on. A wide swath of open green grass stretched out before them, flanked on all sides by thick growths of trees. "It's huge. We would never be able to make enough to unpoison it all."

"Unpoison?"

"You know, stop the poison. Cure it. Unpoison."

Jim nodded.

They sat and thought.

"Maybe we just need a little," Jim said. "Just enough to clear a path so we can get through it."

After a moment of pursed lip contemplation, Toby nodded. "Maybe, but then what? Even if we can somehow clear a path, *they* are still out there." He paused. "Waiting." He stared out into the distance. "Waiting for us."

Jim scanned their surroundings, studying the poisoned land that now encircled them. "I don't see them, do you?"

"Just because you can't see them doesn't mean they're not there."

"I know, I know." Jim looked back to their surroundings. "But do you see them anymore?"

"I thought I saw one over there. Behind that row of trees." Toby pointed to his right.

"A big one?" Jim bit at his lower lip.

"No, I think it was a scout. He looked a lot smaller and his claws weren't so big. And he moved really fast, too. The scouts always move really fast. I saw him behind one of those trees, then all of a sudden I saw him over there behind those." Toby motioned with a toss of his head to a row of trees to their far left.

Jim nodded. "That's fast."

"Damn straight. Super fast."

Quiet again settled around them.

"And besides," Toby said. "You forgot one thing."

Jim looked at him.

"We don't have the ingredients for an antidote anyway. We would need galla root, elenberries, and probably a dozen other things." He pointed into the distance. "We can only find that stuff out there, beyond the trees."

Jim nodded a soft nod, grimacing. "What do you think they want with us?" he asked after a moment.

"Come on, Jim. You know the answer to that."

Jim frowned, but nodded. "Do you think they would prefer us cooked or raw?"

"Does it matter at this point?"

"Yeah, it does. Cooked means I'm already dead. Raw means I might still be screaming when they start chewing."

Toby was pensive for a moment. "Yeah, I hope it's cooked. Unless of course they boil us alive."

"Oh, great. Thanks." Jim threw his hands up in the air. "Thanks a lot for putting that into my head."

They sat quietly for a long moment.

Toby scanned the surroundings, moving his head back and forth, looking, searching. The expanse of green just below them was still, devoid of any movement, empty of any life. They were about fifteen feet up on the wooden platform, close enough to be uncomfortable by the nearness of the tainted earth, but far enough away from the poison to feel a little sense of safety.

"It's really quiet out there," Jim said. He studied the surroundings as well, slowly looking left, then swiveling his head to the right.

"Probably because they are planning their attack," Toby said. "I thought I heard some grinding noises."

"Grinding noises?"

"Yeah. I think they might be sharpening their teeth against the stones."

"What? Sharpening their teeth?"

Toby nodded. "Yeah. They use rocks like whetstones." Toby curled his upper lip back which thrust out his teeth. He moved his finger along his teeth while turning his head left and right. "They rub them back and forth on the rocks. That sharpens them. Some of them can bite a hole right through your bones even."

"Or like right through our skulls?"

Toby nodded. "Talk about a helluva headache, right?" he said and smiled a grim smile.

Jim didn't smile back. "Maybe we should make a break for it," he said. He glanced down at his bare feet. "We could tie rags over our feet, block the poison from seeping through just long enough for us to race through it."

Toby shook his head. "They'll still catch us. If there's anything I'm certain of, it's that. They are fast." He raised a finger for emphasis. "Way faster than us." He glanced at Jim. "Well, way faster than you."

Jim was quiet, ignoring the insult bait. "I don't want to be eaten alive," he said.

Toby suddenly bolted upright out of the chair. He quickly moved to the edge of the platform and stood at the wooden railing that ringed the platform, his hands gripping the narrow wooden beam. "They're closer now."

Jim joined him at the railing, his eyes wide. "Where?"

Toby pointed to a closer group of trees to their right. "Over there. Right behind that weeping tree."

Jim followed Toby's pointing finger to look at the tree with long thin branches and stringy leaves. The leaves drooped down all the way to the ground, shielding whatever was behind them in murky shadows. "That's close, man."

Toby nodded. "Too close for comfort."

"They could be hiding behind all those branches right now," Jim said.

"Not could. Are. They *are* hiding behind those branches."

"You sure the shields will hold."

"Pretty sure," Toby said.

"I thought you said they would hold for sure," Jim said.

"Look, I don't know if they can stand a repeated attack, okay? They should hold, but..." Toby shrugged.

Jim looked out at the weeping tree in the distance. "This isn't good, Toby. This isn't good at all."

⁂

"They're savages, Jim. They can't be reasoned with."

"We need to do something. Anything. I'll go crazy if we gotta stay up here much longer." Jim walked to the right end of the deck area, then turned around and paced back in the other direction. He stopped and looked at Toby. "I can't take much more of this, Toby. We gotta do something." He raised his shaking hand up to the level of their eyes. "Look at that."

Toby stared at Jim's shaking fingers. "Damn, you got it bad."

"I feel like everything's closing in on me. I feel like I'm starting to suffocate. Like some kind of wall is creeping closer and closer, cutting off all my air."

Toby's eyes went wide.

Jim saw his startled expression. "What? What is it?"

"Do you realize what you just said?"

"What? The wall closing in?"

Toby shook his head. "No, the air. Cutting off the air." He looked out at the expanse of land, then up into the sky. A few white clouds dotted the sky in random shapes. A slight breeze ruffled his hair. He glanced back down. "What if they start to poison the air and push it towards us? They poisoned the land all around us, so why not the air, too?" He paused and looked at Jim. "What if it's like carbon monoxide?"

Jim frowned at him.

"You know. It's got no smell or anything. You don't even know it's there until it's too late." Toby paused. "What if our next breath is suddenly our last breath? We wouldn't even know it. We would just suck it in and fall over dead."

Jim put his hand over his throat. "That's terrible." He started to gasp, but brought himself back under control. His breathing came a little faster now, a little more nervous. "Can they do that?"

"Man, I hope not. Then we are really screwed."

Jim resumed his pacing, his hand gently massaging

his throat.

Toby watched him move back and forth across the platform.

Jim paused when he reached Toby. "You said they won't stop hunting us until they get at least one of us." It was more of a statement than a question.

Toby looked at Jim. "That's what I think."

"Then we should probably decide who's the least valuable."

Toby squinted at him. "You mean like vote someone off the island?"

"Yeah. Kind of like that." Jim continued pacing.

Toby thought for a moment. "Well, that's easy then. I vote you off."

Jim spun around and pointed at him. "And I vote you off!"

Toby laughed. "Ha, it's a tie." He glanced back into the dark opening of the small structure behind them. The structure was nothing more than four wooden walls and a slanted roof. It was situated at the back end of the platform. The doorway was small, barely enough room to let one person enter at a time. It was bare bones, but it did at least provide them some relief from the hot sun during the midday heat. He looked back at Jim. "I guess he gets the tie breaker vote."

They both were still for only a brief moment, then both shook their heads simultaneously. "No way."

"There has to be a way out of this," Jim said. He stared out at the open land before them. Time was passing slowly, but the tension in both their faces was growing quickly. He reached the far edge of the platform, spun on his heels and headed back in the other direction. The sun still shone hot and bright in the sky above. Beyond the platform, everything was quiet in the wide expanse of green beyond. A soft breeze made the tree branches in the distance slightly sway to and fro.

"There is," Toby said. "I know you don't want to think about it, but there *is* a way out of this."

Jim was deathly still for a long moment. "You're not suggesting…" Jim shook his head. "No, we can't do that."

"We're surrounded by poisoned land that we can't cross, and even if we did somehow unpoison part of the land, *they* are out there. Just waiting for us. They need to grant us passage. That's the only way out of this. And they only want one of us."

Jim said nothing for a moment. "You said you *thought* they only want one of us. You said you weren't a hundred percent sure about that."

"What else do we have to go on?" Toby asked.

Jim had no reply.

"They're savages, just like we talked about, right? Savages understand sacrifice, don't they? They sacrifice stuff all the time. Cows and pigs and sheep. All that stuff," Toby said. "They'll understand a sacrifice. It means we respect them and fear them."

"Damn right we fear them," Jim said.

Toby nodded. "And it's probably only a matter of time before they stop being cautious of us and come right for us and take what they want. Take *who* they want."

Jim shook his head. "They can't penetrate the shield."

"And what if the shield fails?"

"It won't."

"You can't say that," Toby said. "I told you I wasn't sure the shield would hold. Besides, it happened on Regulon Five. I bet they thought their shield would never give out either."

Jim frowned at Toby.

"Their shield went down and look what happened to them," Toby said.

"What did happen to them?" Jim asked.

"They got eaten," Toby added. "Every last one of them. Every man and every woman and every child. Even the little babies. The whole colony got wiped out."

Jim grimaced.

"What if they come for you?" Toby said. "What if they choose you? What if they pick me?" Toby shook his head. "I don't want them to pick me."

Jim shook his head sharply. "I don't want them to pick me, either," he said.

"Then *we* should be the ones who decide. Not them. Eff them."

Jim nodded. "Eff them."

"We're out of supplies, too," Toby said. "You know that, right?"

"I thought we had some stuff left. Some protein bars or something, no? Some peanut butter and some bread?"

Toby shook his head. He pointed to a wrapper on the platform floor. "He ate the last one."

Jim frowned and looked at the dark entrance to the structure behind them. "No wonder he's taking a nap."

"Yeah."

They sat quietly again for a moment.

After a long moment of obvious contemplation, Jim shook his head. "No, that's just crazy."

"It's the only way to appease them," Toby said.

"Appease them? What the hell is that?"

"You know, make them happy. Give them what they want. If we give them what they want, maybe they'll let us pass."

Jim nodded. "Appease," he said. "We need to appease them. Okay, yes."

Toby suddenly pointed over Jim's shoulder with a sharp stab of his finger. "Wait! I saw one behind that tree over there!" Toby pointed to a grouping of trees to his left.

Jim whirled to look. "Another scout?"

Toby shook his head. "No, way too big for a scout. He was probably about eight feet tall. Maybe ten."

"The hunters." Jim stared into the distance. His expression grew solemn. "The hunters are here," he said. He put his hand to his head, rubbing his fingers over his hair. "Oh, man. Now what? The hunters know were here. I don't want to be eaten alive. I don't want to be boiled like some human lobster."

"The shields will hold. The shields will hold." Toby muttered the phrase over and over and over. "The shields will hold."

Jim turned to look at him, lowering his hand away from his head. "They're not going to hold, are they?"

Toby looked at Jim with eyes that held little glimmer of hope.

Jim's hands trembled with more severe quaking. "Okay, we can't wait anymore. We need to do this. We need to do this now."

Toby looked at him, then slowly turned to look at the dark entrance. They moved for the dark opening and went inside.

They fumbled around in the darkness until Toby managed to light a candle. The pale light emanating from the candle illuminated the sleeping body of Fred Feldman. He was curled up into a ball on a tattered mattress in the far corner of the room. His glasses were still on his face, resting askew across his nose and cheek. The soft sounds of his snoring were clearly heard in the small room.

Jim held up a rusted butter knife. "This?" he whispered. The candle light glinted off the dull metal.

Toby shook his head.

Jim set the knife back down on the small table situated just inside the doorway.

Toby moved over to a pile of sticks and branches amassed in a corner. He reached down and grabbed a sharp-tipped tree branch. It was like a mini-spear. He grabbed another tree branch and held it out towards Jim. "Here, this one's sharp. I told you these would come in handy someday. I wasn't just whittling these for my health."

Jim stared down at the tree branch, then slowly reached out to take it from Toby. "How?"

Toby squinted at him. Tiny shadows flickered across his face from the wavering candle flame.

"How are we going to do this?" Jim asked. He shifted the stick from his left hand to his right hand.

"At the same time. Just stab as hard as you can. Right in the gut. I'll do the same."

"I don't know…"

"It's the only way. Those hunters want human blood. That's what we need to give them." He looked down at the sleeping body before them. "Better him than us, right?"

Jim said nothing. He glanced down at the stick in his hand. "Are we sure about this?"

"You want to be boiled alive? I sure don't."

They both held their pointed weapons at the ready, aimed at Fred's belly.

Toby looked at Jim. "On three, okay?"

Jim nodded grimly.

Dark pools of shadow formed under Toby's eyes. "One."

Jim re-gripped the stick, nervous sweat glistening on his brow.

Toby put both hands around his branch, gripping the stick firmly. "Two."

Jim licked his dry lips, his trembling hands clutching at the sharp stick.

Toby's eyes grew narrower, darker, determined. He drew his sharp stick back further, ready to strike. "Three!"

"Lunch time!" a voice called out from the distance. "Mac and cheese!"

The boys whooped and let go of their sticks. They scrambled back outside into the sunlight and clambered down the rickety wooden ladder that led to the ground below. They raced away from the treehouse towards an open patio door.

Lucille Draper stood in the patio doorway, wiping her hands on a dish towel. She was Toby's mother, a pleasant looking woman with curly blond hair. "Where's Freddie?" Lucille asked as they approached.

The boys looked at each other, slowing as they approached Toby's mother.

"Toby, where's Freddie? Were you mean to that boy again? I told you to be nice to him. You wanna grow up to be a bully? Or worse?" Lucille stared at the two boys as they emerged out of the shadows of a nearby tree and into the bright sunlight. A stricken look filled her face with terror. "Is that blood all over you?"

Inside the treehouse, blood seeped out from underneath the fresh sacrificial corpse of Freddie Feldman.

Outside the treehouse, a woman screamed.

TERRORSTORY #13
POOL OF LIGHT

"Come on! You can make it!"

Rita Mendez shook her head. She was a pretty girl in her late twenties, with long black hair, gentle cheekbones, and a soft round curve to her chin. "I can't!" She looked across the parking lot to the circle of light that radiated down from a light pole. Her friends Sergi and Vanessa stood in the pool of light, waving at her. Her chest tightened. It seemed like it was a hundred miles away. Her eyes were telling her it was only a few hundred feet, but her brain was screaming at her not to believe it.

Rita was still having a hard time processing what was going on. It had only been a few minutes since they had all come out of Louie's Pub, laughing and joking like they always did. Vanessa had pinched Sergi's butt through his black dress pants, promising him some fun when they got home. Rita had been feeling especially good herself because she had made a new friend and hopes were high they were going to share some sweet loving later. She had forgotten her purse in the booth and she and Tori, her new friend, had run back in to get it. When they had come back out, the blackness seemed to have engulfed everything, separating them from Vanessa and Sergi. And now she was trapped in a pool of light surrounded by a terrifying blackness.

Just run. Run as fast as you can. Rita shook her head violently at her own inner voice. *No, that's what Tori did and she never came out of the blackness. She was still in there. God, she was still in the black! Tori was still lost in the black.* Her heart pounded in her chest.

"Come on!" Sergi shouted.

"No! Where's Tori? She's still in there!" Rita held onto the light pole with a fierce grip, hugging it with a desperate hold. The pools of light in the parking lot were the only safe places to be. Everything else around them was dark and dangerous. And black. A deep unending black.

"You can't stay there by yourself!" Vanessa shouted.

Rita looked at the deep blackness that surrounded her. It made no sense. How could she see Sergi and Vanessa in the distance when the black swallowed up everything that entered it? It was like you could see through the black only when you were outside of it. Tori had gone into the black, giving in to Sergi and Vanessa's urgent coaxing. Rita tried to stop her, but

Tori wouldn't listen. Tori pushed her away and bolted into the black. The black swallowed Tori's body as she entered it; the click-clack sound of her high heels on the parking lot pavement just cut off as she stepped out of the circle of light and into the black.

And she was still in there. Tori never reached Sergi and Vanessa. The black had swallowed her up.

The parking lot light above Rita flickered and then went out, plunging her into complete darkness. *My God, I'm in the black!* The air was immediately thicker and she had to struggle to take a breath. Blackness surrounded her everywhere she looked. There were no stars visible in the sky. No streetlights. Nothing. No lights at all. The only things that gave off any illumination were the monstrous beasts that floated in the black all around her. They had a soft white glow to them, making them visible in the dark depths. The creatures swam about, their long tails curling back and forth as they glided through the black. They were swimming in the black like it was an ocean.

One of the creatures turned towards Rita, as if just noticing her. Its black eyes were rimmed with a blue light. It started to swim straight towards her, its mouth opening as it drew closer, revealing several rows of razor-tipped teeth.

Another creature, this one with a long sinewy body and red-rimmed eyes on long stalks, also turned towards her. It slithered like a water snake as it headed for her.

The razor-teeth creature drew closer quickly, its jaws opening even wider. The snake creature was right behind it, catching up fast with quick gyrations of its long thin body.

Run! her mind screamed. *Run where? There was*

nowhere to run. The creatures were everywhere.

The snake creature passed the razor-teeth monster and its jaws opened wide as it neared Rita's face. It had four huge fangs, fangs far bigger than the chompers on the razor-teeth creature. It hissed as it struck for her cheek.

And then the parking lot light flickered back on and the creatures vanished.

Rita heard a loud sound ringing in her ears and only realized after a moment that it was the sound of her own scream. She hugged the pole, stomping her feet up and down. "No, no, no!" she sobbed.

Any lingering effects of the apple martinis she drank at Louie's Pub were long gone. The terror she felt had dried up any alcohol that had been in her system. The adrenalin had completely erased it. Her mind raced. The night had started out so promising. Tori was sweet and so hot with a very nice chest. Her long blonde hair and perky little mouth instantly made her want to taste her lips. Rita liked blondes. A lot. She immediately wanted to know if the drapes matched the sheets. She was pretty certain they would and she just knew Tori would be neatly trimmed down there. Trim and ready for her fingers and her mouth.

Rita remembered the TV that had been playing above the bar. She had noticed it over Tori's shoulder when Tori turned to the bartender to order them another round of martinis. She couldn't hear any sound from the television, the bar was far too loud for that, but she did see an odd news story flash by. Something about a disruptive solar wind finally reaching the earth's atmosphere. The scrolling words warned of potential power outages and possible havoc to electronic devices.

And then Tori had turned back to her, apple martini in hand. Rita remembered Tori's fingers brushing up against hers as she handed her the glass. It was such a simple thing, a simple touch, but she still remembered the excited thrill it gave her. And now that poor woman was out there in the black.

The black.

What the fuck was the black? It was a name that just came to her. *The black.* What the fuck could cause something like that? A solar wind? No, that was no solar wind that struck the Earth. It was some kind of dark energy wave that ripped right through the good ol' planet fucking Earth, ripped a hole right through the atmosphere and filled it up with whatever created that wave, bringing all the monsters along with it. It was as if the Earth was suddenly submerged into an ocean of black goo and the pockets of light were the only thing keeping the black from completely engulfing the planet.

How the fuck do you fight that? It would be like fighting against an ocean. There was no way you could beat that. How the hell do you fight an ocean full of monsters? *You don't.* How many millions had already died? How many millions of people across the globe had the monsters devoured? She couldn't even comprehend the magnitude of it. *Maybe it's only happening here in Indiana,* she thought. But Rita had a sick feeling in her gut that it was happening everywhere.

Above her, the light flickered again. Rita only caught a glimpse of the black this time before the light powered back on. She didn't see the snake creature or the razor-teeth monster anymore, but she saw more monsters swimming in the inky darkness. There were definitely more of them. She thought of sharks circling their prey. My God, they *were* circling her. Just waiting for their opportunity to strike.

She really had to pee. She criss-crossed her legs, holding it in.

Rita looked over at her friends Sergi and Vanessa. They weren't shouting at her to cross over to them anymore. They stood huddled together, staying away from the edge of darkness that encircled them. The light above them now flickered and then went out. They disappeared into the black.

It was only for a moment, but it was enough.

Enough time for a creature to bite Sergi in half. Rita saw his torso-less body fall to the ground when the light above them came back on. Blood sprayed everywhere, spattering Vanessa with red streams of Sergi's fluid. Vanessa shrieked, throwing her hands over her face. Her red dress didn't show the blood, but her bare arms and legs did. They were quickly stained nearly as deeply red as her dress.

Rita saw Sergi's legs flop and kick, striking Vanessa again and again. Vanessa kicked back at Sergi's grotesquely dancing legs, stepping away from them. Stepping towards the edge of the circle of light behind her.

"Vanessa, stop!" Rita screamed.

Rita watched helplessly as Vanessa lashed out furiously at the disembodied legs, the momentum of Vanessa's strike throwing her friend's arm back into the black. Her arm just hung there for a long moment, in the black up to her elbow. And then Vanessa was savagely yanked into the black, pulled right out of her shoes with a vicious jerk from whatever creature had a hold of her arm in the black. She didn't even have time to scream before the black swallowed her up.

Rita just stared at the pool of light across the parking lot that once held her friends. She was too terrified to scream. A soft whimper came from between her lips. "Jesus save me. Jesus save me." Sergi's legs slowed their grotesque twitching, then stopped. Rita wished they would have flopped into the black, but they hadn't. Sergi's severed legs remained within the safe confines of the circle of light, just inches from the black curtain that kept Hell at bay, the ravaged limbs still very visible in the pool of light that streamed down from the light post

Hell. Was that what was happening? Was Hell now on Earth? Was Earth now a living Hell? Is that what the black is? It didn't matter. She was fucked every which way she looked at her situation. And she really had to take a helluva piss.

Rita couldn't hold it any longer. She moved to the other side of the pole, pulled her panties aside and squatted, relieving herself. *God, that felt good.* She finished and moved back to the side of the light pole where she had been standing. Her legs ached so she moved to a sitting position. Movement on the ground startled her. She looked down to see a thin stream of liquid flowing next to her. She immediately stood up and watched her urine flow past her. *Great. I'm all alone at the end of the world, standing in my own piss. What a way to go. Good job, Rita.* She watched the stream flow into the black and disappear.

The light above her again flickered and went out. Rita saw a creature on the ground only a few feet away from her, greedily lapping at her urine trail with a thick tongue. The creature suddenly stopped drinking and looked up directly at her. It studied her for a moment, cocking its head to the side like a dog hearing a shrill whistle. Then it went back to licking her urine. The parking lot light came back on and the creature vanished back into the black.

Was this happening all over the world? Were there other people trapped in a pool of light just like she was? Surrounded by ungodly monsters from some other dimension. *Maybe they were from some other planet. Maybe this was some kind of attack. Some kind of alien invasion.* She shook her head. It didn't matter. She was trapped no matter what the explanation.

Rita saw another group of people in the far distance. They were standing beneath a streetlight on Braum Avenue. They were all huddled tightly together. There were too many of them to fit into the pool of light. She could seem them jockeying for a better position away from the edge of the light. Away from the black. One big man shoved his way through the people, pulling a woman along with him. Rita couldn't hear them, but she could see the others gesturing at him, their mouths open in yelling positions. The big man gave a little guy a shove and the little guy's head snapped back into the black.

The little guy's head never came back out of the black. A geyser of red erupted out of his headless body, spraying everyone in the tight circle of light with his blood. They all jerked about, throwing their arms up, stepping away from the decapitated body, trying to shield themselves from the spurting blood. Several people in the group stepped into the black, or had an arm or hand get pushed into the black. They disappeared in a matter of seconds. One man's hand went into the black and his body was jerked into the black so quickly it looked like he had just been shot out of a slingshot.

Within seconds about half the group was gone, taken by the black. Rita counted seven people left. The big man was still there, one burly arm wrapped tightly around the streetlight pole, his other arm holding his woman tightly to his chest. *Was he a murderer?* For some reason, that question immediately came to her mind. *Was that big man a murderer for what he just did, for shoving that man so his head went into the black? Or was it the only way to save himself and his woman? Did that justify it?*

And who's going to care, Rita? Who the fuck is going to give a shit about that? The black is going to get us all.

Where was the car? She couldn't remember where they parked. She looked left. Was it over there? *Shit, I don't remember. Didn't matter. Sergi had the keys.*

Car headlights appeared on the street in the distance, their beams the only thing visible in the black. Rita couldn't see the car, only the twin beams of light shooting forth out of the headlights. The lights raced down the street. "Hey!" she cried out, waving her arms, but then immediately pulled her arms down, fearful of accidentally putting part of her arms or hands into the black. "Hey!" But the lights just raced on, and eventually disappeared as they turned a corner and headed away from her.

Shit. Rita hugged the light pole. *Now what? I just stand here and die?* She looked at the pool of light in the distance where her friends had been. It was closer to the street. *Yeah, little good that did Sergi and Vanessa.* Still, it was closer to the street. Closer to traffic. Closer to someone who might stop and rescue her. *Yeah, right,*

Rita. Who the hell is going to rescue you? Mommy and Daddy are resting peacefully in their graves. You got no boyfriend because you're a bonafide dyke. You got no steady girlfriend. Your two best friends are dead. Who the hell is going to rescue you? Everybody else is trying to hang on to their miserable life just as much as you are.

Life. Her life. What the hell had happened to her life? She thought about the last ten years and struggled to remember any of it. It was full of work, stress, and TV. A little hanky panky once in a while, but nothing to write a memoir about. That was about it. Every muscle in her body suddenly ached. She felt like she was back at her desk just waiting for Larry to scream at her again about something stupid and unimportant just so he could feel important. *Fucking a-hole. He wasn't even worth thinking about.*

And then Rita saw the most wondrous sight she had ever seen in her life. A hint of a golden red light starting to form on the horizon. The sun! The sun was coming up. *Sweet Jesus of mercy, the sun!* She wanted to laugh. Trapped in a parking lot surrounded by monsters from another dimension and the sun was coming to her rescue. The cavalry riding in at the last moment to save the damsel in distress. She wanted to cry out and sing. But she just watched silently, too exhausted to physically celebrate.

The sunrise strengthened, reaching out farther and farther into the black, pushing the darkness away.

The parking lot light above her went out. But she didn't care. The sun had reached her. The black was gone. It was gone! Rita hugged the pole, the lingering fear of the black still gripping her. The parking lot was still half full of cars, but no one else was in sight.

Did that really just happen? *Maybe somebody slipped*

something into my drink, she thought. *Yeah, that had to have been it. Somebody drugged me.* She closed her eyes and hung her head, shaking it slowly. *Jesus, I'm never going to that fucking bar again.*

For a brief moment, she saw the monsters from behind her closed lids. One of them stared straight at her, its mouth open, the tips of its razor-teeth glistening. Rita threw her eyes open as a startled gasp exploded out of her mouth. *What was that? Jesus. I must have fallen asleep.* But something inside her doubted that. She hadn't fallen asleep. The monsters were there in the black. In the blackness behind her closed eyes. *No. I fell asleep,* she thought. *I fucking fell asleep. I was dreaming. Some asshole in the bar dropped some shit into my drink and this whole thing is just a weird dream.*

But then Rita saw Sergi's severed legs, the blood splatters on the ground, and she knew that it had been no dream. She saw a large wet smear of blood on the parking lot pavement about a dozen feet away and she just knew that was all that was left of Tori. One of Tori's charm bracelets lay on the ground nearby, coated in blood. Noises sounded in the distance and Rita realized they were sirens. The blaring blasts of alarm came from all directions. It sounded like the world was ending. *Maybe it is.*

Rita looked over at the other group in the distance huddled beneath the streetlight. None of them had moved away from the light yet. The big man still held his woman tight against him. They all stood still near the light pole, just looking around.

Would the black return tonight? She already felt certain of the answer to that question. It would be back. Rita knew it would be. And so would all the creatures who live in it. Did the black cover the entire world? Was every night going to be like this? She glanced at a deep pool of shadow near the corner of the bar. Even though the sun was out and rising, it wasn't reaching everywhere. There were still shadows everywhere. She stared at the dark area near the bar. *Was that a tiny pocket of black? Were the monsters swimming in there right now?*

Rita looked over at Sergi's legs. Were his car keys still in his pockets? *I have to get home. I have to prepare. Lamps. I need more lamps in my apartment. And light bulbs. Fuck, I need a shitload of light bulbs. And coffee. I need coffee coffee coffee.* She forced herself to be calm. *I have time. The day just started. I can make it. Just stay out of the shadows. Just stay out of the black. I can make it.*

Then why aren't you letting go? She ignored the questioning voice and kept her arms wrapped tightly around the parking lot light pole.

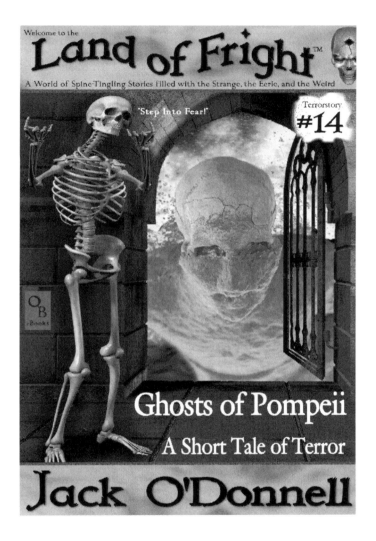

TERRORSTORY #14
GHOSTS OF POMPEII

"Are there bodies still in there?" Cal asked.

Victoria Carlsin glanced down at her son. Cal was eight years old with tight brown curls. He had his father's brown eyes. Sometimes, Victoria thought of getting him colored contacts so she wouldn't keep seeing Harold in Cal's face.

Antonio, their Pompeii tour guide, smiled a tired smile. He shook his head. "No, there are no bodies in them," he said. Antonio was a tall man with dark black hair and a nose on the larger side. Definitely an Italian. Victoria could see it all over his features.

"It's like they are frozen in ash," a frumpy woman in their tour group said.

What a weird expression, Victoria thought.

Victoria was forty-two years old with tight cropped black hair. Very business-like in manner and appearance. She ran a flower shop in her small town where she handled every aspect of the business from the ordering of product, to advertising, to social media marketing. She did it all. And now she was taking a well-deserved break on a vacation to Italy. Frozen in ash, she thought. But what the frumpy woman had said was true. Their bodies did look frozen into position. They looked like statues made of solidified ash that contained a once-living human being. Victoria stared at the mass of bodies on the ground.

"This is the Garden of the Fugitives," the tour guide said. "From their position in the ash, archaeologists believe these thirteen people died on the second day of the eruption as they attempted to flee the city."

"The second day?" someone asked.

Antonio nodded. "Yes. They had no way of knowing that the eruption was about to enter its deadlier phase. Super hot toxic clouds of gas and debris blasted down the slopes of Vesuvius and overwhelmed Pompeii, killing everyone who had not yet left." Antonio looked back at the bodies. "Killing them."

Victoria looked at the statues on the ground. One of them she could clearly see was in the shape of a child. It was laying on its side, near a larger adult shape. A few feet away from them was a statue of what was once clearly a man. He was the most tragic figure of the group. He was not lying flat and curled up like many of the others; his upper body was off the ground with his right elbow pressed against a mound of earth and his left hand on the ground, pushing himself up in a supreme effort to rise. He was frozen for all eternity in that position. Trying to get up.

"Archeologists found these victims in the hardened layers of ash and volcanic debris. They filled them with plaster to create these statues you see before you. They are just plaster body casts."

Okay, so there were no actual remains hidden within the ash shapes, Victoria thought. Still, the whole tableau fascinated her. It would have been sorely disappointing to come to Pompeii and not see a body frozen in ash. Isn't that why she had wanted to come here? To see the bodies? To gaze upon the poor souls whose lives were snuffed out in a matter of moments by the violence of nature that no one could control. If Mama Nature wanted to spit up red-hot molten puke, no one could tell her otherwise. Victoria snorted but held in her laughter. Was that all an eruption was? The aftermath of Earth's hangover? An upset core spewing out some nagging bit of unpleasantness from its stomach? Earth barf? A squeak of laughter came out of her mouth despite her attempts to hold it back.

The tour guide frowned at her. "Something funny about the dead, miss?" Antonio asked.

Victoria looked at him, hiding her mouth with the back of her hand. "No, no."

"I've been doing this tour for twenty years and no one has ever laughed before. Not here." He looked at her quietly for a long moment, then turned away.

The tour group moved on, leaving Victoria and her son standing alone before the plaster statues. Victoria stared absently at the departing tour group.

She felt her cheeks flush with embarrassment.

"Wait until you see Herculaneum," someone in the group said.

"Why?"

"They have hundreds of these frozen ash bodies. The entire town was covered in ash. It got hit worse than Pompeii did when Vesuvius erupted. There's a whole bunch of gladiators. Even a lot of animals intended for the arena to fight in the games. Tigers and stuff."

"Wow, that's cool."

Victoria watched the tour group move away. I didn't mean to laugh, Victoria wanted to say. But she kept silent. No one paid her any attention.

"Look, Momma, it moved," Cal said.

Her son's voice pulled her out of her thoughts and Victoria looked away from the tour group. "What, honey?" She looked at her son.

Cal pointed to one of the ash statues. "He moved. That one moved."

Victoria frowned. "They can't move. They're dead. There's not even a body in there. You heard the man. They are just shells in the shape of people. They're full of plaster."

"No, he moved. I saw him move."

"Now, Cal, that's just not possible, honey. Don't make up lies like that. Your teachers don't like it when you do that at school, and I don't like it when you do that with me. You promised you would try, remember? No more stories."

"It's not a story. He moved."

"Cal." Her tone was clearly a warning to him.

"Mom, he moved!"

"Now, Cal, you stop it."

"He fucking moved!"

"Cal! Watch your mouth! I'm going to wash it with soap when we get back to the hotel!" She looked up at the tour group in the distance; no one was looking in their direction. She turned back to Cal and tugged on his arm, pulling him along behind her. "I'm going to wash that nastiness right out of you. Let's go. The tour guy is leaving us behind."

"And despite what you may have seen in certain movies, there were no gladiatorial games being held on the day Vesuvius erupted," Antonio said. "We know from inscriptions that no games were scheduled for that month."

Victoria looked at the tour guide. He had avoided looking at her ever since her silly snort accidentally came out of her mouth.

"As a matter of fact, that day was a day of devotion. It was a religious holiday devoted to the opening of the Roman underworld. If they were not attending sacrifices in the Forum, most Pompeians were expected to stay home and indoors while the spirits of the dead roamed abroad."

They stood in the central market square of Pompeii as the tour guide continued. Several stone columns towered up a few dozen feet on their right. Numerous other column bases dotted the area. Several buildings with crumbled walls were visible on their left. The towering mountain of Vesuvius dominated the background. People once stood where she stood, Victoria thought. People who laughed, smiled, cried. People who once were thriving and alive. It was an odd feeling. Both exhilarating and profoundly sad all at the same time. Why don't you laugh again, you idiot. She ignored the biting voice.

"Mom, I have to go to the bathroom," Cal said.

"Just hold it. I think we're almost done."

Cal looked nervously over his shoulder, back in the direction they had just come.

Victoria followed his gaze back towards the Garden of the Fugitives. "Really, Cal. Knock it off."

Cal took one final look back over his shoulder, then looked back at her. He fidgeted, crossing his legs. "I really have to go."

"We'll go back to the hotel after this, okay?"

Cal nodded. And looked back over his shoulder again.

<hr />

"Oh, Cal, honey, get off there." Victoria shooed him off the hotel bed and pulled the top bed cover off the bed. "That's disgusting. Who knows what kind of germs are on there." She folded the top bed cover down to the end of the bed. "There, sit on the sheets. I know they changed those."

She glanced at the uneaten snack on the desk nearby. "Aren't you going to eat your cannoli? It's got some chocolate in it, I think."

"Nah. I'm not hungry."

"Tired?"

"Yeah."

"Did you have fun?"

"It was okay."

"Go ahead and hit the sack. I'm gonna jump in the shower and go to bed, too."

It was the pleasing promise of a warm shower that drew her into the bathroom. It was the chilling cry of her son's voice that made her race out of it.

Victoria raced out of the bathroom, a towel loosely draped around her body; her hair was still lathered with the white foam of shampoo. Her heart pounded in her chest. "Cal?"

Cal sat huddled on the floor, crying. He kept trying to touch his arms, but then just cried out again.

She bolted over to him, crouching down next to him. "Cal, what is it? What happened?"

"He burned me. That man burned me."

"What? What man?" Her gaze darted about. The door to the hotel room was closed. Victoria quickly glanced left to see the patio door was open; the curtain ruffled slightly in the breeze. She quickly moved to the patio door and glanced outside for a brief second, but saw no one. She slammed the door shut and locked it. She raced back to Cal. "What happened? Did he hurt you?"

Cal nodded.

"Who was it?"

"The ash man." Cal looked up at her with a face streaked with tears. More tears poured out of his eyes. "I told you he moved!" He raised up his arms and she could see the burns seared into his flesh. It looked as if someone grabbed his forearms with burning hot gloves; the markings of individual fingers were clearly evident as red welts on his flesh.

Victoria fumed. *I can't believe they threatened to send me back home to the States. What the hell is that about?* She had stormed out of the police station with Cal in tow right after they told her that. *Like hell I'm going back home. I spent three years saving for this trip. I'm going to fucking enjoy it.*

They switched hotels and were now staying in a smaller place a few miles away from their first hotel. There was no way she was staying in that other hotel. The people at the Espladia didn't want her to make a fuss with the police about the break-in so they offered to pay her hotel fees for the rest of the week. She didn't object.

No one could explain the burn marks on Cal's arms. They made no sense. The emergency clinic had patched him up, slathering his burns with cream and bandaging them up in gauze. They gave her a prescription for some pain medicine. She hated to give Cal medicine and avoided it as much as possible, but she knew he was going to need it for this. Those burns were going to hurt for quite some time before they healed.

Victoria thought about the look the nurse had given her in the clinic. *Like I'm some nasty woman who burned her own son!* She looked at me like I was a complete loon.

How the hell did he get those? It was just crazy. The room had an iron, but it wasn't turned on or even plugged in. It didn't have a kitchenette or a microwave either. *How on earth did he burn himself? On what?* The burn marks did look like fingers. Like someone grabbed him with hot metal gloves. *Or with hands made out of burning hot ash.* No, that's just not possible.

Victoria looked over at Cal sleeping on the bed. The medication looked like it had knocked him out. Good, she thought. He needed to rest. Maybe they should just go home, she thought. How was Cal going to enjoy the rest of their trip with those burns on his arm? He's going to be miserable.

How the hell did he get those? She couldn't wrap her mind around it. How the hell did he get those burns? The question would not leave her head.

"Mom, I don't think we should be doing this," Cal said. He wore a long-sleeved shirt to protect the bandaging that was now covering his burn wounds. "It's trespassing." He fought back a yawn.

Victoria shushed him. She felt guilty for waking him up. She knew he was exhausted, but she couldn't leave him alone in the hotel room. "Just be quiet." She glanced over her shoulder, but didn't see anyone in the area. She motioned at the small fence that surrounded the tour area they had visited earlier. "Go, climb over it."

"My arms hurt," he said.

Her face softened. "Come on, I'll help you."

She helped Cal climb over the fence and then quickly followed. She nearly tore her blouse on the fence, but managed to unsnag it before the fabric ripped.

They both stood in the darkness, hiding near the corner of one the building walls. The moonlight shone down on an ancient stone street of Pompeii. She could see the stone steps that protruded up from the ground in the middle of the street. The ancient

Pompeians used them to cross the streets so they didn't step in the filth and dirt and animal dung that littered their streets.

"It's over there," Victoria said as she pointed down the street. "Cross over the stones and turn right."

"We shouldn't be doing this. I just want to go home."

She shone her smartphone out in front of them to light the way. "Let's go."

Cal followed her onto the street, not bothering to step on the stone protrusions. He suddenly stopped in the middle of the street. "Mom!" he hissed.

Victoria stopped in the middle of the street and glanced down at him from where she stood on a crossing stone. "What?"

"I saw someone!"

She moved off the stone and crouched down next to him. "Where?"

Cal pointed into the distance down the street. "I saw someone crossing over the street up there."

She put her smartphone face down against her jeans, stifling the light as best she could. "Are you sure?"

"I think so."

"Was it a security guard?" she whispered.

Cal shook his head. "I don't know. Just somebody crossing over on the stones."

"They were on the stones? Are you sure?"

"Yes."

For a brief moment Victoria wondered why a security guard would bother to cross the street on top of the stones? Maybe it was just a younger guard playing around. She grabbed Cal's hand and tugged him forward. "Come on."

❖

"See, Cal, he's still there. He didn't move." Victoria pointed to the figure of the man lying on the ground struggling to get up for all eternity. They were back at the Garden of Fugitives, staring at the plaster body statues on the ground through the protective glass.

"Yeah, but where are the two that were over there?" Cal pointed to a spot off to the right.

Victoria aimed her smartphone in the direction of his pointing finger. The soft light coming from the phone illuminated the space he pointed to. It was empty. The ground around it was clearly disturbed. Where were they? She didn't have to wait long before she got her answer.

They were right behind them. Their heat gave them away.

Victoria and Cal both turned around slowly at the same time.

The two ash figures stood before them. Red and yellow glimpses of light appeared from within their bodies, the light shining through tiny cracks in their ash shells. It was lava. Victoria just knew it was. It was molten lava moving inside them. Their eyes glowed with red heat. She could feel the heat pouring out of them, washing over them in a hot blanket of air. The air started to feel thick, started to darken as if filling with soot all around them. She glanced down at the feet of the ash figures to see a dark cloud of smoke swirling about their legs.

She remember what the toured guide had said

about the day of the eruption. It was a day when spirits of the dead roamed abroad. Is that what these things were? Ghosts of Pompeii walking the streets? Using the hardened bodies of ash as their vehicles. That's madness, she thought. That's just not possible. Yet here they stood before them. "Please," she said. "Please don't hurt us."

Victoria thought she heard a sound issue forth from the ash man's mouth. It sounded like a sniggering laugh.

The ash man standing before Victoria reached out and grabbed her wrist. The pain was fiery and hot as the thing's hand immediately scorched her flesh. She opened her mouth to scream but the pain was so intense only a desperate whimper came out. She felt her eyes rolling up in her head. Her brain felt as if it were going to burst into flames at any moment. The heat was beyond anything she had ever felt before in her life. The ash slid down her fingers, and further up her wrist and up her forearm. The heat was excruciating. It felt like her flesh and bones were melting. She could smell the hairs on her arms burning. She heard a crackling noise and realized it was her own flesh starting to char and crack.

Victoria fought to stay conscious. She struggled to turn her head to find her son; her entire body shook and trembled with extreme agony. She finally managed to turn her head enough to look over at Cal. He was already half consumed by the ash creature standing in front of him. He wasn't making a sound. His eyes were open but they did not move. The thickness moved up his neck and over his face, sealing her son inside the dark gray ash.

The ash continued to move up Victoria's arm,

disintegrating her blouse as it reached the fabric, coating her shoulder, moving to her back.

She opened her mouth to scream.

"You are a lucky group." The tour guide pointed out two bodies frozen in ash to the throng of solemn tourists gathered around him. The name embroidered on the tour guide's shirt was Antonio. "These two bodies were just discovered during a new excavation. We believe it was a woman and her son caught trying to flee the city. The deadly poisonous smoke and ash storm must have caught them by surprise. It's rare to find remains of people actually standing like this. It's quite a find."

"It looks like she's screaming," someone commented as the group marveled at the ashen statues on display.

"She certainly isn't laughing," Antonio said.

"Are there bodies in there?" a young girl in the group asked.

The tour guide smiled.

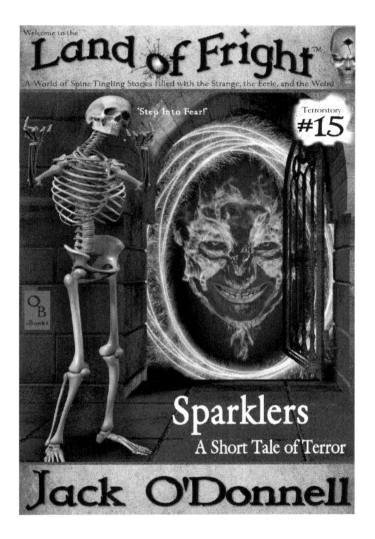

TERRORSTORY #15
SPARKLERS

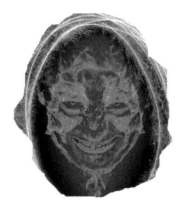

"Daddy, look at the circle I made."

Dan Miller looked up when he heard his daughter's voice. He was sitting in his usual solitary position, part of their annual 4th of July party but a distance removed. He was in his late-thirties, his paunch growing out a little bit year by year as the amount of exercise he did diminished. He had set up his lawn chair in the front yard, dozens of feet away from the stinging smoke of the grill. Everyone else was seated near the grill, or milling around near the silver metal cooker. The evening was starting to take hold as the sun set in the distance.

Dan glanced to his right, looking for Suzie. Several of the neighborhood kids were lighting snakes on the sidewalk, jumping around excitedly as the charcoal black bodies spewed forth from the tiny pellets, twisting and writhing as they expanded. He saw two of his nieces and his nephew with them, but not his daughter. He casually tipped the beer bottle to his lips and took a sip. The beer was starting to get warm and had an unpleasant bitter bite to it. He wasn't a big drinker, so he already had a slight buzz from his first beer and felt comfortably lazy in his lawn chair.

"It's beautiful," he heard Suzie say.

Dan looked to his left and saw his wife talking with her sister. They were deep in their usual animated conversations, hands flailing as they talked in that Italian woman kind of way. *Jesus, did they ever stop talking?* A few more kids stood near them, waving their sparklers with absolute glee.

Then Dan saw his daughter. Suzie stood very still. The sparkler she clutched in her tiny ten-year old hand was now nothing but a thin piece of metal with a charred tip. Suzie was very petite for her age, her long blonde hair hanging straight down the back of her white party dress. She held the sparkler stiffly at her side, as if her arm was frozen in that position. Dan set his beer down and rose up out of the lawn chair, moving towards her. *Damn sparklers*, he thought. "Hey, Suze, you okay?" he asked as he reached her side. "You burn yourself?"

Suzie didn't answer. What she did next sent an odd chill racing up his spine. She slowly raised the dead sparkler, pointing the tip away from her, her arm moving slowly as if she were pushing it up through thick syrup. Dan followed the direction she was pointing in and the chill intensified.

Dan stared at a thin circle of light floating in the air. It shimmered and glowed. He took a hesitant step closer. It was the glowing trail left by a sparkler when it was whipped through the air. The trail usually lasted for but a few brief seconds before it faded away. But not this trail. It lingered. It hung in the air. It was a complete circle, its thin edge golden and bright. He leaned closer to it, peering at it. Its center was completely black. Dark, deep, and devoid of any light.

Until the large eye appeared in its center and blinked.

Dan jerked back, startled by the abrupt appearance of the huge orb. He opened his mouth to cry out but no sound came out. He stared at the large eye in the middle of the golden circle. It was an eye full of emotion. Rage. Hate. He could feel it emanating from the eye. He suddenly felt paralyzed. He willed his muscles to move, but he remained as still as a statue.

He only moved after a clawed hand shot out from the circle of light, grabbed his daughter and pulled her into the blackness. Then, he moved. And then Dan screamed. "Suzie!" He jerked towards the circle, hitting the rim of light with his hand. The light immediately faded, vanishing into nothingness.

The circle was gone. His daughter was gone.

"Suzie!" Dan circled the area in the front yard where his daughter had just been standing, waving his arms frantically, spinning round and round, shouting his daughter's name over and over. "Suzie!"

The others came racing over to him.

"What's wrong?"

"What the hell are you doing, Dan?"

"What's going on?

Dan clawed at the empty air. "Suzie! It took Suzie!"

His wife came to his side, grabbing his arm. "What? Where's Suzie?" Linda asked. She was a thin woman with short-cropped blonde hair, dressed in white shorts and a pink halter top. She looked at Dan with a dour face.

"It grabbed her. It grabbed her!" Dan shouted, his voice rising.

"Who grabbed her?" Linda pulled on his arm tightly. "Who? You're scaring me, Dan. Where is Suzie?"

Dan jerked his arm out of her grip. "It took her. That thing in the light took her!" Dan threw his hands to his head, grabbing at his thinning hair. "Oh my God, oh my God." Suddenly, he dropped to the ground, clawing at the dirt. He lifted up a dead sparkler. "This." He looked at the strip of metal in his hand. The sparkler seemed thicker than a normal sparkler. The color at the tip looked more like dried blood than blackened soot. "Who brought this?" Dan asked. He got to his feet, frantically shaking the sparkler stick. "Who brought these? Where are they?"

"What are you talking about?" Linda's voice grew tight and firm. "Dan, where is Suzie?"

"It took her, damn it. I told you that." Dan looked at the crowd of family and friends gathered around him. He raised the sparkler. "Who brought these?"

"It's just a sparkler," someone said.

"It's not just a sparkler." Dan clenched his jaw. "Who the fuck brought these?" He saw trails of light in the corner of his vision and saw some of the kids still waving sparklers. "Stop!" he shouted. "Stop them." He hurried over to the children. He reached one of the small neighborhood boys and slapped the sparkler out of his hand. The boy started to cry. The sparkler continued to spit out tiny bursts of light. Dan grabbed the sparkler from the ground and started to make circles in the night air. The edges touched, forming a complete circle, but the light faded. The sparkler died a moment later. Dan threw it to the ground.

He spun and yanked a sparkler out of one of his niece's hands and start making circles in the night air. Round and round he waved the glowing, sparking stick. The light circle stayed lit, but only for a few seconds, and then the circle of light faded away.

Dan moved towards another girl with a sparkler, but a strong hand grabbed his wrist, stopping him. He looked up to see his brother-in-law Rodolfo staring at him. "What the hell are you doing, Danny?" His voice was sharp, but hushed. Rodolfo was a big man with big hands. He had a thick black mustache and a gleaming bald head. A tattoo of a cobra adorned his right arm.

Dan tried to yank his hand away from Rodolfo, but Rodolfo had a firm grip on his wrist. "It took Suzie," Dan said. "It took Suzie."

"What the fuck is wrong with you?" Rodolfo asked. "Suzie is right here."

Dan looked up at him. He blinked. "What?"

"Hi, Daddy."

Dan slowly turned to look at his daughter. Suzie waved a quick wave at him, smiling. Behind her, a golden circle seem to hang in mid-air. "Oh my God."

Dan hurried over to her and pulled her into a crushing embrace. "Suzie, oh my God."

Behind them, the sparkler circle of light faded away.

Suzie put her arms around him and leaned closer to his ear. "He's coming for all of you," she whispered.

Dan quickly jerked back from his daughter, holding her at arm's length.

Suzie smiled and nodded.

Dan took Suzie's arm and pulled her away from the crowd that had gathered around them. Linda came over to them. His wife took Suzie's arm and pulled her towards her. Dan held firm on his daughter's other arm.

"Let go, Dan," Linda said.

"You let go." His voice was icy cold and full of firm resolve.

His wife let go.

Dan looked down at Suzie. "Who was it, Suzie? Where did you go? Who did you see?"

"What are you doing, Dan?" Linda asked. "What the hell is wrong with you?"

He looked at Linda. "I saw something grab her. It pulled her right into the circle."

She frowned. "What circle?"

Dan waved his hand. "The circle. That damned sparkler circle."

His wife's frown deepened. "How many beers did you have?"

"One. And I didn't even finish it."

Suddenly, Dan bolted away from them, slapping away at the air, disrupting a circle of light that his niece had just swirled in the night air from her sparkler. "Don't do that!" He moved to another child nearby, waving and slapping at the light trails the boy was making.

His wife yanked on his arm sharply. "Dan, stop it. You're scaring people."

Dan turned sharply to Linda. "Good. They should be scared."

Linda stared at him. "Let's go." She turned to look back at her daughter. "Come on, Suzie. We're going home."

"No we're not," Dan said.

"Yes. We are."

Dan shook his head. "No, we are not." He spotted a circle of light hanging in the air. The light did not fade. He pushed past his wife. "Get away from it!" He hurried over to the circle of light, pulling his nephew Ritchie away from the glowing circle. Dan ripped the sparkler out of his nephew's hand and stared at it. The handle of this sparkler was similar to the one Suzie had been holding. It seemed thicker than a normal sparkler. He looked at the darkened tip. It was a dark red, not black like it should have been.

"Where did you get this?" Dan asked his nephew.

"From that pile over there," Ritchie said and pointed. No one even looked at where he was pointing. Ritchie didn't even look in that direction either. Everyone was too entranced by the shimmering circle of light that hung in the air.

Slowly, everyone gathered around the glowing circle. Questions. Disbelief. Shock. Fear. Dan felt the emotions behind the jumble of questions spilling forth from the people around him, but he didn't hear any of the actual words.

Dan shoved the sparkler into the dirt, dousing the

flame.

Suzie was suddenly standing at his side. She pointed at the circle of light. "He's in there, Daddy."

"Who's in there, Suzie?" Linda asked. Linda's face was filled with fright. She could barely speak and the words came out in a slow halting way. Her fingers trembled. "Who's in there?"

"I think it's God."

"I don't think it's God. Look." It was Dan's sister-in-law Trish speaking. She pointed at the circle with a trembling hand.

The eye was back. Watching. Staring. Malevolent.

A huge clawed hand reached out from the black depths of the circle, snatched Ritchie, and pulled him into the darkness. Screams filled the air. The circle vanished.

"You call the cops?"

Rodolfo nodded. Dan could see that his big hands were shaking. "They said half a dozen people blew their hands off with firecrackers, so they're real busy. Someone will get here when they can."

"That's more important than my kid being missing? They need to fucking get here now!" Trish demanded.

"I know. I told them," Rodolfo said.

"Fucking tell them again!"

Dan heard them continue talking but tuned out their words. He stared at the pile of sparklers on the ground. He looked up. "Where did these come from?"

Everyone just gave him shrugs and head shakes.

"Nobody brought those?"

More head shakes.

Dan slowly reached down and picked one up. The metal was cold. He looked up at Rodolfo. "Light it."

"You sure you want to do that?" Rodolfo asked.

Dan glanced around the yard. All the children were inside now, staring at him from the front window. He looked back to Rodolfo. "Just light the fucking thing."

"All right." His brother-in-law flicked his lighter and lit the end of the sparkler.

It spat and sputtered like a normal sparkler, throwing off tiny sparks and glittering gems of light.

Dan waved it in the air, making a wavy line in the night air. It felt like an ordinary sparkler in his hand. He thought he would feel something, some kind of weird tingling or something, but he just felt the cool metal in his hand. He listened closely. *Was that voices? No, it was just the crackling of the sparkler. Wait, was it voices?* He wasn't sure. The sound was very faint.

He rotated the sparkler, but he moved it too slowly. The circle did not reach the other end. It faded before the ends touched. He swirled the sparkler faster in a big arc, making a full wide circle, a much larger circle than the kids had made. It nearly touched the ground and reached up to nearly his full height. The ends touched and joined. The circle remained full, the edges bright.

"My God," he heard someone mutter.

Dan stared at the circle of light hanging in mid-air. And then he stepped into it.

For a moment, everything went black. Then, Dan's vision returned. There was a dim glow coming from in front of him in the distance. Dan turned to look back and saw his brother-in-law on the other side of the circle, but Rodolfo was a shimmering kind of image, wavy and surreal. Ghostly.

Dan looked at the house and could see everyone looking at the circle. They, too, were wispy and pale like vaporous phantoms.

He glanced up the street. Everything was tinted with white and black edges in some kind of weird impressionist painting tableau.

"Ritchie!" he shouted. He glanced around. "Ritchie, are you here?"

And then Dan saw his nephew as the light in the distance grew brighter. Ritchie was sitting in the lap of some hideous demon on some kind of bizarre throne made of bones. The creature was big, twice the size of a man. Its flesh looked thick, leathery. And it appeared sunburnt, a deep red, or like some kind of ancient parchment was stretched over its body and then splashed with blood. It looked as if the beast was chewing on Ritchie's head; its head was bent over, its mouth very close to Ritchie's ear. Ritchie laughed at the demon, nodding his head. The demon pulled back and gently patted the top of his nephew's head with its large claw. It had been talking to him, not eating him. Ritchie beamed the creature a huge, happy smile.

"Ritchie!" Dan raced toward them.

The demon slowly looked up as Dan approached. It gently moved Ritchie off its lap. The demon looked at Dan and patted its lap, motioning for Dan to come over to it. It was like some sick Santa Claus from Hell. *Christmas in July,* Dan thought, and almost laughed at the madness of it all.

A crackling noise drew his gaze and Dan realized the sparkler was still burning in his hand. He tossed it to the ground and moved closer to the demon. He urgently wanted to sit in its lap. He desperately wanted to hear what the creature had to say.

He tried to focus on the thing's face but it kept shifting, shimmering, changing. *Was that his father's face? No, now it looked more like his mother's face.* They were both dead so it made him wonder if this was some unearthly portal into the next life.

Suddenly, Ritchie wasn't there anymore. Dan glanced around, but did not see him. The demon gently patted its lap again. Dan moved towards it and climbed right into its lap. The demon's legs felt warm, comforting, reassuring. The demon put a gentle arm around his shoulder and started to whisper in his ear.

And then everything made sense. The eye they had seen in the sparkler circle of light had not been full of rage and hate. It was full of love and compassion and understanding.

And hunger. Hunger to save him. Hunger to save the world. Dan could feel the hunger coming from the demon as if it were a palpable layer of flesh covering its body. It was more than just a craving; it was a ravenous need that demanded to be satiated.

Dan was part of something, the creature explained. Something bigger than himself. Part of a whole that wasn't yet complete. It wasn't an odd sensation to feel incomplete; Dan had felt that way his whole life. Like an outsider, like someone who didn't quite fit in with everyone else. He didn't really mind it anymore. He had just accepted it. But now the feeling was different. The emptiness inside him seemed to be like a vast chasm filled with despair. He didn't want the abyss to be inside him anymore. He wanted it to be filled. He wanted it to be filled with love.

Dan felt a slight tingling in his neck. A slight sting. A bit of a pinch. Maybe the demon was feeding on them after all. Dan didn't care. Didn't a priest feed on the beliefs of his parishioners? Didn't a rabbi feed on the faith of his flock? Didn't a minister feed on the prayers of his followers? The demon had given him a purpose. The demon had saved him from a life of isolation without meaning. After all, without purpose, what was life?

A sudden understanding burned inside Dan like a hot flame. He knew his purpose. And he knew he had to share it with everyone else. They had to know what they were missing. There was no choice involved here. They needed to know. They needed to see. They needed to feel what he felt. Dan knew Suzie already understood. He now understood the little gleam he had seen in his daughter's eyes. She was happy. She had a purpose. As did he.

Everyone needed to know. Strangers. Friends. Family. Rodolfo. Linda. Everyone. They had to have faith in the truth that was now revealed to him. Even if it meant forcing them to feel it. How could he deny them that? It just wasn't right to deny anyone this feeling. It was downright immoral. He knew some of them would fight him, resist him. They just wouldn't understand until they felt it for themselves. He couldn't let them remain ignorant savages blinded to the truth. They all needed to enter the circle and be saved. How could he rest knowing others were not part of this— this glory?

Glory. It felt odd to think of the word. Glory. It

was a strange word. A word he had never used before in his entire life. But now it fit. Glory. No, not just glory. Rapturous glory. That was even more fitting.

The demon pointed to a pile of sparklers nearby.

Dan climbed down from the beast, immediately missing the warmth and comfort of its lap. He turned around to see the demon standing upright, its beautiful red wings unfolding out from its back. In that moment, Dan knew he had been so wrong. This was no demon. This was no demon at all. It was an angel. An angel sent to rescue them all.

Dan took the sparklers and headed back towards the circle of light where he had entered this new wonderful world. So much to do, so little time. So many people to send into the circles.

After all, angels needed to eat, too.

Dan glanced down the neighborhood street. Gleeful laughter filled the air. A string of firecrackers went off. A haze of blue smoke from a smoke bomb filled one yard. A bottle rocket zipped high into the sky and burst with a faint pop. A tiny cardboard tank scooted across the sidewalk and its little muzzle fired a few feeble shots before it burst into flames. And dozens of sparklers crackled and twinkled, their glimmering trails weaving and floating in the air.

"Uncle Dan, look at the circle I made."

Dan looked over at the glowing circling hanging in the air in front of Ritchie. All around him, other circles formed. Many circles. Circles leading to glory. Circles leading to hungry angels.

"Me, too, Daddy."

Dan turned to stare at the circle shimmering in the air in front of Suzie. He smiled at his daughter and lovingly patted her head. He handed her some sparklers from the pile at his feet. "Go show your friends."

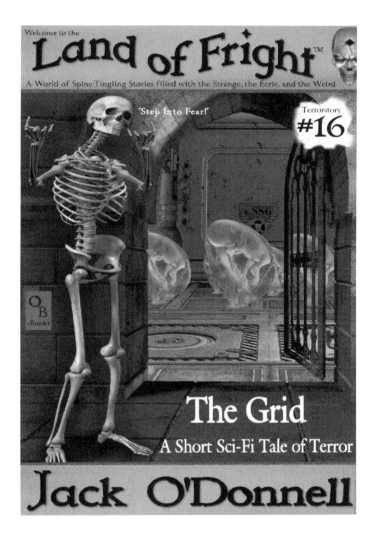

TERRORSTORY #16
THE GRID

"**I**t's some kind of grid," Grim Jorgens said.

"Is that what the criss-crossing sets of metal bars on the floor are?" Breen Noreen said. "As always, thanks for your keen insight." Breen was a thick man with a thick face. His black hair was cut short atop his head, giving his head a flattened appearance. A lifetime of ridicule over his rhyming name had taken its toll on his psyche, so his attitude towards others was often curt and condescending purely as a defense mechanism.

Grim frowned at him. He was taller than Breen, his face longer and narrower than his friend's. Grim had close-cropped hair as well (short hair was so much easier to manage in the zero-g environments they spent most of their time in), but his hair was a light shade of brown. "Okay, wise guy, what's it for then?"

Breen looked down at the metal grid. They had searched several corridors already, looking through rooms as they went along, but found nothing worth salvaging. The grid was the first really interesting thing they had come across since boarding the vessel. The surface of the grid was raised slightly higher than the corridor floor, situated on a platform. The bars were very thin, forming a fine mesh that covered a square area of the floor. A dark control panel was situated on the wall to their right. "Some kind of transporter device, perhaps?"

"Transporter? What the hell is that?" Grim asked.

"Are you really unfamiliar with the concept of a transporter? It often amazes me how you are able to function at all."

"You know what *never* amazes me? How much of a dick you are," Grim said.

Breen continued as if Grim had not spoken. "It disassembles your atoms on this end, beams you through space, then reassembles you at some other location. Quite a fascinating imaginary concept, but one that has never been achieved in reality."

"Yes, fascinating." Grim paused. "Only to you."

"Let's see if it turns on." Breen moved over to the panel and studied it for a moment. He stared at a piece of reflective metal on the wall near him and caught a reflection of himself in the gray surface. He looked at himself for a long moment, turning his head slightly left, then right. He licked his fingers and pushed down a few unruly tufts of hair with a few pats of his fingers. He turned to Grim. "Get on." He motioned with his head toward the platform.

"So you can beam me through space?" Grim shook his head. "Uh, no fucking way."

Breen touched the panel and it immediately blazed to life. He took a quick step back. "Hello." The grid crackled and glowed white hot for a brief moment before cooling down to a dull shimmer.

"And you wanted me to stand on that? Really? I'd say that was a bad suggestion, wouldn't you?"

"My suggestions are neither good nor bad," Breen said. "They are merely suggestions. Which course of action you choose to follow is entirely up to your judgment."

"Breen," Grim said and paused. "Sometimes I want to smack you silly. If you hadn't saved my ass on Deltair Five, I wouldn't have given you this job."

"And if I also had not saved your ass on Trebulan, you would not be breathing the stale air of this fine vessel," Breen countered.

They both stared at the glowing grid.

"So what is it?"

Breen and Grim nearly leaped out of their suits as Valri Carlok stepped up behind them. She looked at the two men, a wide pleasant grin lighting up her slender face. She was suited up in a dull white spacesuit just as they were, her helmet and gloves also clipped at her side. Her hair was cut even shorter than the two men, with a slight reddish tint to the very thin layer that covered her head. She had a generous mouth and a clearly mischievous glint to her green eyes.

"Shit, Val, don't do that," Grim said. "I thought you were taking a nap?"

Valri looked at Grim and shrugged. "Nah, decided to join you two fuckheads." She glanced around the area, looking up the corridor she had just come from, then down the hallway to the left of the grid. She had picked up the stray alien ship on their scopes days ago. It was just floating dead in space. There was no sign of any recently active propulsion system. No heat signatures. Nothing to indicate it was still a working ship. "What kind of ship is this?" she asked.

Grim shook his head. "We don't know. It's not Slektali or Dendru. And I don't think it's Terran."

"It's Nalarian," Breen said. His tone had a definitive finality to it.

Valri glanced at Grim and he just rolled his eyes.

Breen pointed to a marking on a nearby corridor crossbeam. The symbol was several slashes intersected with a whorl. "That's Nalarian."

Valri looked at Breen. He wrinkled his nose and stared right back at her. She looked down at the grid. "Kind of out of place on a Nalarian ship, don't you think? Looks too high tech for those slugs."

Breen frowned at Valri. "Are you wearing that foul perfume again?"

"Grim likes it." Valri smiled at Grim and gave him an affectionate bump with her shoulder.

"Me like lots." Grim reached over and kissed Valri, awkward as it was with the bulk of their suits getting in the way.

"I have absolutely no idea what she sees in you," Breen said and turned away.

"Yeah? Well, I know what I see in her," Grim said.

Breen turned back to look at him.

Grim patted his crotch and grinned.

"You nasty boy," Valri said and gave Grim a

playful smack on his cheek. She looked back at the shimmering metal grid. "So what is it?"

"Genius thinks it might be a transporter," Grim said.

"Hmm," Valri said, her gaze staying fixed on the grid. She moved up to the edge of the grid and unhooked her helmet from her belt. She stared down at the grid for a moment, helmet in hand.

The men remained quiet.

Valri bent down and set her helmet down on top of the grid, then took a step back.

They waited for a reaction.

Nothing. The helmet just sat on the glowing grid.

Valri picked up her helmet and studied it for a moment. She ran her fingers along the helmet's rim. "Nothing. Not even warm." She clipped the helmet back on to her belt. Then she stepped up onto the grid.

"Hey!" Grim shouted and reached for her arm, but it was too late. Valri was already standing on the grid.

Valri turned around in a few small circles, staring down at the grid. She looked up at the two men. "Nothing." She stepped off the grid to stand between the two men.

Breen sneezed.

Crackle. The grid started making noises.

They all slowly looked down at the grid.

Crackle. Crackle. Crackle. Tiny pinpoints of light burst up from the grid in hot flashes. *Crackle. Crackle.* The bursts of light came from all over the left side of the grid, in front of where Breen stood. A few bursts came from the center of the grid and one or two from the far right of the grid.

"What the hell?" Breen muttered.

The tiny points of light started to grow, taking on solid form. They had a pinkish color to them. A flesh color. They watched, rapt with fascination, as the globules grew larger and larger. The three salvagers slowly moved back away from the grid.

"No..." Valri said. The word came out in a slow gasp.

"What?"

"Is that... a..."

"A what, Val?"

She turned to look at Grim with wide eyes. "A fetus." She looked back to the largest of the growing forms. "Is that a fetus?"

"What?" Grim studied the growing shapes. "No, I don't think it's a fetus. Wait, shit, it does look human. Look, it has arms and legs now. They're growing. Damn, they are growing fast."

"Does that look like me?"

Grim and Valri turned to Breen.

Breen slowly extended his arm and pointed at the largest of the shapes near the front of the grid. "That looks like me."

Grim and Valri turned to follow his pointing finger. "Holy fuck. It does," Valri said.

They all stared with disbelieving eyes at the growing life forms.

"What the hell is going on?" Breen muttered.

No one had an answer. They stood still, a dozen feet away from the grid now, watching the life forms continue to enlarge. Several of them were at least a few feet in length now. And they all bore an uncanny resemblance to Breen.

"Your sneeze," Valri said suddenly.

Breen scowled at her. "What?"

"Your fucking sneeze. You sneezed on the grid."

"So?" Breen frowned.

"So? So you basically spit your DNA all over it."

"What?" Grim said.

Valri looked at Grim. "He spit his DNA all over the grid."

"So?"

Valri pointed to the beings on the grid. "So, it's taking that information and replicating it."

"Shit, it wasn't a transporter. It was a replicator," Grim said and slapped his forehead. He smiled.

No one else did.

Breen suddenly raced forward and jumped onto the platform. He raised his booted foot and brought it smashing down on one of the things, stomping on one of the forms closest to the edge of the grid. It exploded with a sickening squish. Blood splattered everywhere. *Crackle. Crackle. Crackle. Crackle. Crackle. Crackle.* More flashes of light erupted from the grid where the blood splashed. More bodies started to take shape. A lot more bodies.

"What are you doing?" Val shouted.

Breen moved about on the grid, stomping and smashing. More blood splashed everywhere as the creatures exploded beneath his heavy boots.

"Stop!" Valri grabbed Breen and yanked him off the grid, jerking him away from the menagerie of half-formed bodies and twisted growths.

Several of the shapes rolled off the grid and lay on the corridor floor, writhing and squirming like grotesque, over-sized worms. Bursts of light erupted forth from the grid in a blinding flurry of flashes. More embryonic bodies appeared, took form and grew. They filled the large grid to its capacity, spreading across its entire surface. More of the bodies rolled off the grid, spreading out into the corridor.

Grim, Valri, and Breen backed up away from the grid at a much quicker pace.

⊰⊱⊰⊱

"That just leads to the stardrive. We can't go that way," Grim said. He stepped back into the corridor from the darkened room and re-joined Breen and Valri. The creatures had replicated so quickly that they blocked off the only path back to where their ship was docked. They now urgently looked for another way off the alien ship.

"It's cloning me or something! We have to stop it." Breen said.

"The only thing we have to do is get the hell off this ship," Grim said.

In the distance, they could hear movement. And the same question repeating itself over and over and over. *"Does that look like me?"* It wasn't coming from Breen's lips. It was coming from the replicated versions of him. Sometimes the voice was deep and throaty. Sometimes the voice was high and shrill. Sometimes the voice was a thunderous shout. But it was always unnerving and savagely irritating. *"Does that look like me?"* The question never stopped. It echoed in the narrow corridors and never had a chance to fade away before the question was asked again. *"Does that look like me?"*

"Any weapons in there?" Valri asked, motioning with her head to the room that Grim had just exited.

Grim shook his head.

"Anything that even looks like a weapon?"

86

Grim shook his head.

"Does that look like me?"

"Anything we can rip off the walls? Pipes. Chair legs. Anything?"

"No. It's all bolted hard in place."

"Does that look like me?"

Breen threw his hands over his ears, squeezing his face tight, jamming his palms against his head.

"Does that look like me?"

"Yes!" Breen shouted. "Yes, that looks like me! Yes, you look like me!"

The questioning voices stopped.

The three of them froze. Grim cocked his head, listening. Valri stared intently back down the dim corridor they had just passed. Breen slowly lowered his hands from his head. He turned hesitantly to follow Valri's gaze.

"What the hell?" Valri muttered.

"It can hear?" Grim asked. "Do you think it's sentient?"

Valri looked at him, then shook her head unknowingly.

They all stared into the darkness of the corridor they had just run through. They could hear the sound getting closer. It wasn't a sound they had ever heard before in their lives. It wasn't the sound of the voices. It was the sound of flesh tumbling over itself, the sound of skin scraping along skin, skin scraping along walls, flesh scraping along the floor.

Valri raised her flashlight up and shined it down the corridor.

The wall of jumbled bodies appeared in the beam of light, moving closer to them. It was a mad mash of fully formed bodies, half formed bodies, quarter formed bodies, misshapen blobs of flesh. They all had some perverse resemblance to Breen in some manner. Some of the bodies were even fully formed and looked exactly like him. The wall of flesh moved closer, the Breen-thing bodies filling the space from floor to ceiling, tumbling end over end as the mass behind them pushed them forward.

"Isn't this where one of us comes up with the last minute rescue plan?" Valri asked.

"Yeah. I'm all ears," Grim said.

"Maybe we can just push our way through it," Valri said.

They all stared at the thick wall of bodies. There was no space in the approaching mass of Breen-thing bodies that wasn't full of flesh.

"Talk to it," Grim said.

"What?" Valri frowned at Grim.

"Talk to it. It must have heard Breen shouting at it. There's no way that was a coincidence. They heard him."

Valri turned to Breen. "Shit, say something. Talk to yourself. We know you're good at that."

Breen looked up at her. "What am I supposed to say?"

"Shit, anything. Tell it to leave us alone. Tell it to stop. Tell it to go away. Tell it to get the hell out of here."

Breen stared at her for a moment.

"C'mon, Breen, just say something to it," Grim said.

Breen turned to look at Grim, then slowly nodded his head. He turned to stare at the jumbled mass of flesh grotesquely tumbling towards them. One of the Breen-thing bodies spilled over and Breen stared at an exact replica of himself before the moving wall of flesh tumbled over it. "Fuck you!" he shouted, the words exploding out.

The replying answer was strong and firm. *"Fuck you!"* Another voice answered. Then another. *"Fuck you!"* Then another. *"Fuck you!"* Then another. *"Fuck you!"*

"Real eloquent, Breen," Valri said.

The bodies tumbled and churned and rolled closer.

They turned and ran.

The mass of flesh filled the corridor, smashing up against the bulkhead at the end of the hallway. *"Fuck you!"* the voices said. Then a body spurted out of the mass and into the hallway that led away from the corridor at a right angle. Then another body and another. Soon, the mass was again heading down the corridor towards them. Breen's face appeared at one angle on one Breen-thing body, then at another angle from a different Breen-thing body. *"Fuck you!"*

Grim and Valri held hands at the end of the corridor, watching the approaching mass. Breen stood beside them. "What do you want?" Breen shouted.

"What do you want?" a Breen head said. *"What do you want?"* another Breen head said. *"What do you want?"*

That's when they noticed the disturbing protrusions jutting out from many of the bodies. The erect penises of the Breen-thing monstrosities. They pulsed and throbbed and twitched. *"What do you want?"*

"Are you fucking kidding me?" Valri said. She grimaced in disgust and tugged on Grim's hand, pulling him down the next corridor.

<hr />

"There's no way out. The door is sealed shut," Valri said.

Grim pounded futilely on the steel door barring their path. He kicked at it repeatedly, making loud grunting noises as he lashed out with kick after kick. "Fucking open!"

"Grim, it's not going to open," Valri said, her voice firm.

Grim kept kicking.

"Grim."

Grim looked up to see Valri eyeing him with a stern face. He lowered his boot and stared down at the floor. He took a few deep breaths. He looked back up at her. Her face remained flinty. "So now what?" he asked.

The rumbling sound drew closer. They stared at the end of the corridor as the sounds grew louder. *"What do you want?"* And then the mass of the Breen-thing bodies appeared, spilling out of the darkness, pushing around the corner, heading towards them. *"What do you want?"* They filled the corridor from floor to ceiling. They just rolled and tumbled over each other, moving closer and closer. *"What do you want?"*

"Stop!" Breen shouted. "Stop!"

"Stop!" the hundreds of mouths said. *"Stop!"*

Valri reached over and gave Grim a long kiss. He looked at her with a curious expression. She kept her face even as she unclipped her helmet and put it on. Grim watched her lock the helmet in place, then quietly followed her example.

Breen snatched at his helmet and hurriedly slammed it down over his head.

The three of them stood quietly at the end of the corridor as the mass moved closer.

"Stop!" a Breen-thing said. *"Stop!"* said another.

"Isn't there anybody else we can call?" Grim asked. His voice came in over their helmet speakers.

"I already sent out half a dozen distress signals," Valri said.

They were all quiet again.

"Stop!"

"Well, this certainly wasn't the way I expected to go out," Grim said.

"Not looking forward to getting impaled by a bunch of Breen dicks," Valri said.

"The sad thing is you do mean that literally," Grim said.

No one laughed.

The voices of the Breen-things grew louder, closer.

Grim turned his head so his helmet faceplate pressed against Valri's. He stared into her eyes, then opened his mouth to speak.

She shook her head immediately. "Don't say it, Grim. You can tell me later after we get out of this."

The forward edge of the Breen-things reached them. Grim lashed out with his booted feet, stomping several times, crushing the skull of the Breen-thing body at his feet. Blood stained his boot, the floor. He looked up at Valri. "You have no idea how satisfying that was."

Valri and Breen followed his lead, stomping and

kicking at any body that got close, but they were quickly overwhelmed.

A ship waited in space, hidden on the dark side of a nearby moon.

Monitors stationed around the control room displayed the gruesome images of the Breen-things crushing Grim, Breen, and Valri beneath their relentless mass.

"That wasn't expected." The commander of the ship was a tall Nalarian. His speckled brown and white skin was thick and scaly. It was evident he was homeworld born. Most homeworld born Nalarians had thick skin to battle the biting sand-winds of Nalaria. He had no interest in the three salvagers who were getting crushed to death. They were of no consequence whatsoever. They had simply started the process in motion. The speed and volume of the replication were what fascinated the commander the most. "These curious Terrans may turn out to be a very valuable resource indeed."

"We didn't realize they would replicate so quickly. The contents of the sneeze was an added bonus." A technician at one of the stations pointed to a graph on his monitor. A tremendous spike was apparent in the data he was studying by the sharp upticking line.

"Yes."

"And all the blood gave the grid enough genetic components to amplify the replication a thousand fold." The technician pointed to another spike in the chart that was far beyond the first spike in intensity.

"And you are certain it doesn't require those things

to function? Saliva or all that blood?" the commander asked.

"Completely certain. All the replicator needs is a strand of hair, a drop of sweat, the residue of a fingerprint. The Terrans natural curiosity will lead them to investigate every grid they come across. It will only be a matter of time before one of them triggers a response from a grid," the technician said. "And the resulting consequences will be entirely because of their own actions. They cannot possibly blame us."

The commander nodded. "And the talking? Was that expected from the replications? How is that even possible? They are just supposed to be meat, aren't they? Why give them any additional functionality at all?"

The technician looked up at him. "Well, they are Terran, after all. Their kind do like to talk. Besides, that will liven up their deaths, don't you think? Hearing them scream. We thought the Gorgalla might enjoy that as part of its dining experience."

The commander frowned.

The technician clearly read the displeasure in the commander's face. "We can work on programming the grid to leave out any vocal capabilities in the replication process."

The commander nodded. "I think that would be wise. All that chattering will get tiresome rather quickly." He stared up at the monitors, taking in the squirming mass of bodies filling the screen. "The Gorgalla will feed very well tonight."

"You could say it will gorge itself," the technician quipped.

"You could, but I won't." The commander looked

away from the technician, glancing at a separate isolated view screen.

Beyond the ship, floating in space, a massive star creature waited to feed. It was three times the length of the ship. The Gorgalla had its own biological atmospheric generator that enveloped it in a microscopically thin layer of protection from the ravages of the void. Its thick copper skin was in essence its own spacesuit. The Gorgalla's skin looked soft, but the commander knew it was harder than his own ship's hull. Its golden wings were folded against its side.

"Do you think it will enjoy its first taste of Terran meat?"

"I hope so," the commander said. "Now that the Pulsha are practically extinct, what other choice do we have?"

"Stop!" "Stop!" "Stop!"

The full mass of the bodies reached Grim, Valri, and Breen and started pressing against them. They had nothing but an impenetrable steel door behind them, so they had nowhere to go. The Breen-thing bodies kept coming, kept squeezing against them. Arms and legs jabbed at them. The jutting penises poked at them. Knees and elbows pushed against them.

"Stop!" "Stop!" "Stop!"

Valri and Grim stared at each other as the wall of flesh pressed tighter and tighter against them. They each could feel the weight on their chest grow with each passing moment. "Okay, you can say it now,

Grim," Valri said.

Grim started to speak, but their helmet headsets crackled, then went out. He started to mouth some words to her, but the intense pressure caused one of the Breen-things to burst and blood splattered all over Valri's faceplate, blocking her vision. She couldn't raise her arms to wipe it away; the pressure of too many bodies kept her hands pinned to her sides.

"Stop!" "Stop!" "Stop!" The word rolled incessantly out of the Breen-things.

Breen had his hands up near his face. His faceplate was streaked with red smears. He clawed at the approaching bodies, ripping flesh and skin. He tried to kick them back but the mass of bodies pressed against his legs, pinning them to the steel wall behind him. Several Breen-thing bodies pushed hard against his midsection and he had to struggle for every breath.

"Stop!" "Stop!" "Stop!"

The head of one of the Breen-things pushed against Breen's chest and he could feel his ribs starting to crack. And then one of his ribs gave way with a sickening crunch, then another. The head of the Breen-thing kept moving, crushing through his ribs, driving relentlessly forward.

The Nalarian commander stared disinterested at the sight of the Terran salvagers being crushed to death on the ship's monitors. He was still a bit concerned about the volume of replicated meat. It had nearly filled every corridor on the derelict ship. For the most part, however, he was pleased with the test deployment. He turned and headed out of the control room. He moved through his ship, heading for the cargo hold.

He reached the entrance to the cargo hold and nodded to the sentry standing guard. The sentry nodded back and stepped aside, giving him access. The commander stepped into the cavernous room of the cargo hold and paused, surveying the thousands of food farm grids that awaited deployment.

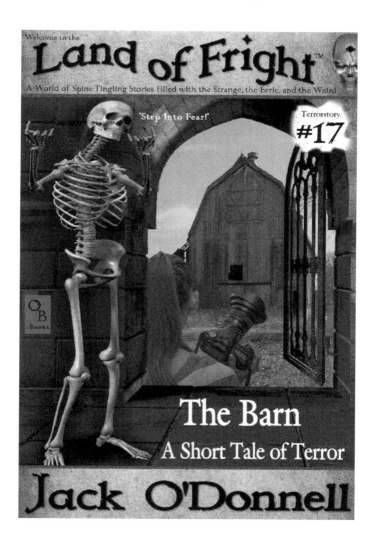

TERRORSTORY #17
THE BARN

The dark windows of the barn stared at Katherine Prezsinksi. The open doorway beckoned her. *It called to her, but she didn't hear it from the confines of her car.*

Katherine fingered the camera resting on the passenger seat of her car. Did she have time? She was supposed to meet Phil at seven when he finished his shift. She glanced at her watch. It was only five-twenty. Fuck it. It was too good of a chance to pass up. Besides, the fading sunset was absolutely beautiful. It was a vibrant reddish orange with subtle wisps of white clouds to give it some visual pizzazz. It gave the dilapidated barn an ethereal glow, with a hint of blood-red thrown in for good measure. Way too good to pass up.

She grabbed the Nikon and headed out of the car. She glanced over at the house in the distance. It looked abandoned. *It wasn't, but it sure looked like it was.* There wasn't even a rusty pickup truck parked in the front yard. Two of the windows were boarded up. The grass was high and unkept. A battered tire swing hung limply from a huge oak tree in the front yard. She was pretty confident no one was around and didn't think anyone would care if she trespassed. *She was wrong.* She snapped off a few pictures of the old farmhouse. She could make the fading yellow paint that covered the old house stand out starkly against the green grass with some HDR software. The photos would make a good addition to her portfolio of photographs on Dreamstime, Shutterstock, and DepositPhotos. She needed a few more good barn shots to complement her other rural photographs.

Katherine turned back to look at the red barn. Yeah, the farmhouse was pretty neat, but that barn… That barn was just spectacular. It was remarkably well preserved in comparison to the dilapidated house it shared the land with. She had a few barn shots in her portfolio, but nothing like this one. She hoped the interior wasn't as disappointing as the last few she had explored. *It wasn't.* The barn had a typical gambrel roof, with two slopes on each side, with the upper slope positioned at a shallower angle than the steeper lower portion of the roof.

She crouched down and framed the barn in her view screen, and then paused at what she saw in her viewfinder. The barn looked like it was grinning. The two dark windows in the front of the building looked like eyes. The old lantern hanging over the door was like a tiny pert nose. And the sagging doorframe gave the hint of upturned lips. The right side of the doorframe was slightly higher than the left, giving the grin a bit of a smirk. Katherine clicked off a few shots. She adjusted the lens to take a few wider panoramic shots. A few bare skeletal trees gave a nice visual edge on the left of the shot.

The dirt road crunched softly underneath her gym shoes as she approached the dark doorway. She stood just outside the barn for a brief moment. She glanced over her shoulder at the farmhouse again, at the quiet empty country road just beyond it. She followed the road for a ways in both directions; there was no traffic whatsoever coming or going. She wasn't quite sure why, but she didn't want anyone, including random strangers, to see her snooping around on someone else's property. She felt guilty doing it, but her curiosity always overpowered any misgivings.

Katherine turned back to the barn. She hesitated on the threshold for a brief moment, staring at the murky depths within the old building. A slight breeze ruffled her short brown hair. *Don't be shy.* Then she stepped inside.

The air inside the barn smelled fresh. Katherine had been prepared for it to reek of dead animals, decay, and moldy hay. But it smelled — clean.

Ahh, yes. Welcome.

It was a pretty big space. The light streaming in from the open doorway behind her helped illuminate the vast majority of the interior, but there were still a few pockets of deep blackness in the distance. To her right were several fragmentary remnants of stalls of some sort, only the metal poles remaining of what were probably once low wooden walls that housed cows. Beyond that, several more stalls were visible; these were more intact, with the majority of their wooden-slat walls still in place.

Outside, the wind picked up ever so slightly.

One of the shutters from an upper window banged shut, pinching off a small ray of sunlight that had been shining through it. Katherine glanced up at the sound, looking at the shutter, then continued moving her gaze upwards. The roof was surprisingly in excellent condition, she noticed. She couldn't see even one hole in it, not even a crack. It was no wonder the interior barn floor looked so dry and dusty.

Come in, come in.

She took a few more steps inside, the camera still down at her side, for a moment forgotten. All of the other high windows were tightly shuttered. They, too, were in surprisingly excellent condition and very finely crafted. Not a sliver of light shone through the rest of the closed shutters.

Katherine brought her gaze back down, noticing all of the windows on the floor level were also tightly shuttered. One of them had a slight crack in it, but the visible strip of light coming through it was so thin it was barely discernible.

She noticed an odd pile of debris in the far back right corner of the barn. *Yes, go see.* She moved towards the pile, passing an old tire on the ground, a rusted pitchfork with its prongs facing downward, a few overturned rusty pails.

She passed the decrepit stalls and paused at the

first stall that still had its wooden-slat walls. She moved to the edge of the stall and glanced inside.

Something scurried in the dark corner of the stall.

No, no, not yet! Not yet.

"Shit!" Katherine was momentarily startled and took a quick step back, but still had the presence of mind to pull her camera up to her eye and click off a few fast photos. The flash went ***pop pop pop*** as she fired off some shots. She glanced at the view screen, thumbing back through the shots she just took. Two of them were photos of dirt, the barn wall, some scraps of indeterminate metal. But one was not.

One photo clearly showed an animal, or at least its tail. Was that a rat's tail? No, it was too big to be a rat's tail. Could be a cat's tail, she realized. It was a bit puffed up so it was probably just as freaked out by her presence as she was by its sudden movement.

Rabies. The word just came to her. What if the damn thing had rabies? She did have jeans on. The thick denim would at least provide some protection. Maybe it was a raccoon. Could a raccoon bite through jeans? Or through her sneakers? Her sneakers were just made of thin canvas. Raccoons did have some pretty damn sharp claws. They were like little human hands. It could probably grab tight on her shoe and chomp down right through it and put a nice puncture bite right in her big toe.

Katherine looked at the photograph in the view screen again, the tiny LCD screen backlight giving it a soft glow. No way that was a rat. The tail was just too big. And didn't raccoon tails usually have circular black rings on them? She couldn't remember. She didn't see any black rings on the animal's tail, but it was too hard to tell for sure with such a muddy picture.

She took a few calming breaths as she stared into the murky corner of the stall. She saw nothing. No more movement. *None that she was aware of.* Whatever it was, it was gone. She thought about turning right around and hightailing it out of the barn, but she didn't. She only had a few more minutes anyway before she had to get going. Come on, don't be a scaredy Kat, she thought. Scaredy Kat. That was Phil's favorite name to call her when they watched spooky movies together. Katherine didn't mind. She played along and pretended to be scared, because then she could snuggle up to him and Phil would put his arms around her and hug her tight.

Might as well at least get a few more pictures. She knew she would probably never pass this way again. At least not for a while, anyway. Who knows if the barn would even still be here in a few months. She waited for a few more minutes as her eyes continued to adjust to the gloom, but she didn't see any more movement. The animal was probably long gone by now. *It wasn't.*

Katherine turned away from the stall and moved closer to the pile of debris she had seen earlier. But as she got closer she realized it wasn't debris. It wasn't debris at all. It was an arranged pile of human skeletons. One skeleton appeared to be sitting up, resting its back against the wall, its bony hand resting on its bony knee. The dark sockets of its skull looked like gigantic black eyes that stared right at her. Another skeleton was on its hand and knees, as if frozen in a scurrying position. A third skeleton was lying flat on the ground, its bony arms positioned tightly against its bony sides.

What the hell? Katherine felt a crawling sensation all along her skin as a nervous tremor shook her body; the hairs on the back of her neck stood straight up. Who were they? She wondered how long they had been there? It looked like they had been there for years, but she didn't really know how long it took for a corpse to turn into just a bony skeleton. Had someone dug them up from a graveyard and put them there? Fuck, now do I have to call the police? Man, I don't want to get involved in that shit. What a weird picture, she thought. Picture. Jesus, Kat. She had again forgotten about the camera in her hand. She raised the Nikon up to her eye.

That's when the barn door slammed shut with a resounding boom. *Hee hee.* The loud sound felt physical to Katherine, as if it were accompanied by a blanket being yanked down over her. A deep blackness engulfed her. Panic clutched at her thoughts, threatening to overwhelm her. She couldn't see a damn thing. Get the hell out of here, Kat. Get the hell out of here now.

She heard a shuffling noise behind her, a scurrying of feet in the dirt. She whirled, raising her Nikon like a .45, and fired off a few shots. **Pop pop pop.** Dazzling flashes erupted from the camera, revealing several animals *creatures* moving towards her. The creatures shrieked and drew back, scurrying back into the dark depths of the barn.

With a trembling hand, Katherine raised the camera and glanced at the view screen. "My Lord…" she managed to whisper. Her heart pounded in her throat. Her chest tightened and her breaths shortened to panting inhales and quick exhales.

They weren't rats. They weren't cats. Not dogs.

Not raccoons. Katherine didn't know what the hell they were. She had never seen anything like them. They were between her and the only exit. She stood motionless, afraid to take a step, afraid to even move. Was that someone else breathing? Or some other thing? She tried to calm her own frightened breathing to listen to the disturbing sounds coming from in front of her, but she couldn't stop her panting. Her fingers shook.

Then Katherine remembered the pitchfork she had passed when she first came into the barn. Where was that? Could she reach it? Maybe she could pinpoint the area where she had seen it. She fired off a shot. *Pop*.

But then wish she hadn't.

There were now half a dozen creatures in the barn, all of them moving towards her. They all shrieked their horrible shriek as the blast of light attacked them. One of them looked like a dog with massive tusks. Two of them looked like cats with huge paws and long leathery tails. One looked like a pig, but instead of a snout it had a mouth filled with tiny sharp teeth. There were larger shapes visible behind those creatures, but she didn't have time to make them out before the light faded. The creatures scurried back away from the brightness.

Her heart pounded in her chest. The air didn't smell fresh anymore. It smelled rancid. And it felt thick; she had a hard time sucking it into her lungs.

Katherine could feel the creatures in the darkness, feel them coming nearer as if their bodies were pushing the air closer and closer to her as they approached. She fired off more shots — *pop pop pop* — sending them scampering back. Their shrieks rang in her ears.

She had to look. She couldn't help herself. She glanced at the view screen. Was that a horse face? Her hand shook wildly. My God. Was that a horse head with teeth like that? And look at that one. What kind of fucking monstrosity was that? That tail looked like it had claws. How could a tail have claws?

Her battery light started to blink. Low battery. Low battery.

Something flew past her head and Katherine gasped. She swiped frantically at it, forgetting the camera in her hand, and clunked herself in the head. "Fuck!" She fired off more shots, just aiming the camera all around her and clicking wildly. *Pop pop pop pop*. The barn filled with bright light and screeches and howls.

The creatures were everywhere. Flying above her. Creeping towards her. There were some crawling up the wall next to her. Katherine backpedaled in a frantic flurry of feet and slammed hard into the barn wall as she gave ground to the approaching horde of creatures. She sidled along the wall, keeping her back pressed tightly against it. She didn't know which way to go but her momentum kept her going to her right. She thought about the pitchfork again but she knew that would not help her get out now, not with this many creatures in her path.

Darkness returned as the flashes faded. Only a feeble red light was visible. Katherine glanced down to see what it was.

Low battery. Low battery.

Something brushed against her shoulder and she whirled away, firing off more shots. *Pop pop pop*. White hot light revealed a serpentine creature moving down the back wall. The creature hissed at her and then vanished into the darkness. She had to make a run for it. Where was the door? She glanced to her right. Was it over there? She looked left. No, over there.

Something touched her leg. Katherine fired shots downward, aiming her camera at the ground. *Pop pop pop*. There was something clutching at her shoe. It was the creature she had seen earlier. The one she thought might be a raccoon. As the blasts of light illuminated the beast, she realized it was some kind of mutant monster, a raccoon-thing with hands double the size they should be. Its mouth was twice as big as it should be. And so were its teeth. It looked up at her with coal black eyes and hissed the most venomous hateful hiss she had ever heard. Katherine shook her foot violently, trying to jar the creature free. "Get off me! Get the fuck off me!" The raccoon creature's grip tightened around her foot. More flashes of light struck the creature as Katherine fired off more shots from her camera. *Pop pop pop*. The mutant raccoon creature squealed and let go, darting away from the blasts of light.

Darkness returned, punctuated only by the tiny red warning light on her camera. And then the feeble red light vanished. The battery in her camera was dead. Katherine felt absolute terror overwhelm her. Phil, I'm scared. This time, I'm really scared.

Now, my friends. Now.

A shrill scream filled the air. Dark shapes stared at the barn from one of the boarded up farmhouse windows, peering out from behind the slats. A gleeful chuckle rang out. "Got us another one."

"Mommy, look at that barn. It looks like it's smiling."

Gretchen Schultz looked at her son in the passenger seat, then out the window where he was pointing. The two big windows in the front looked like big eyes. The lantern hanging over the door looked like a small nose. And the sagging doorframe did make it look like the barn was smiling. "It does, doesn't it?" she said.

"I think it wants us to come in and play." Charlie looked over at her. "Can we?"

Gretchen kept her gaze on the barn. "We have to get home. Daddy and grandma are waiting for us."

"C'mon, Mom. Let's just go see what's inside. Just for a minute."

A beam of sunlight flared off one of the dark windows and then was gone. Gretchen felt like the barn had just winked at her. *Come on in.*

"I bet there's some cool old stuff in there. Maybe some old tractors and stuff," Charlie said.

I bet there is some cool stuff in there, Gretchen echoed her son's sentiments in her thoughts. She glanced at the yellow farmhouse, the old tire swing, the high unkept grass. There was no car parked outside. Some of the windows on the house were boarded up. It looked like no one lived here anymore. Before she realized what she was doing, she found herself turning onto the dusty driveway, heading towards the smiling barn.

"Yes," she heard her son exult. Gretchen saw Charlie pump his fist out of the corner of her eye. She smiled. What the heck? Why not? They never did anything fun together. Just work and school, work and school. An endless cycle of sameness. This would be fun. Even if it was just for a few minutes.

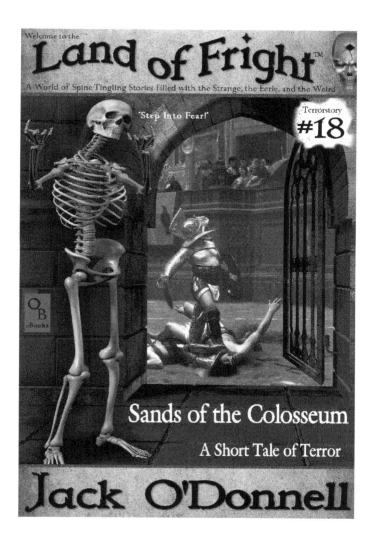

TERRORSTORY #18
SANDS OF THE COLOSSEUM

The sight of a Roman centurion with a smartphone plastered to his ear struck no one as being oddly anachronistic. It was just part of the bustling activity outside the Colosseum that nobody paid much attention to. "He's got it," the centurion said into the phone. "He even paid twenty bucks for it."

"Bello. That's fitting. Our country needs every penny we can get, right?" The voice on the other side of the call laughed. "You're sure he's part of my tour group today?"

"Yep."

"Good. And he has the right one?" the voice on

the phone asked.

"Yes. It's got your dark mojo all over it." The centurion watched two attractive ladies walk past him. He smiled at them and they smiled back. "Gotta go," he said into the phone.

It was going to be the tour of a lifetime, Bob Corwin thought. They were going to walk around the seating areas where Roman senators used to sit and watch the bloody gladiator games. They were going to explore the narrow hallways beneath the Colosseum where the gladiators, and the wild animals, waited their turn to fight. And they were even going to stand on the arena floor, right where all the action took place, the animal hunts, the criminal executions, the brutal gladiator fights to the death.

There was an energy to the place that Bob could not describe. He had felt a vaguely similar feeling on a tour of an Aztec ruin in Mexico City, but nothing like this. He could almost feel the dark history as a tangible presence here.

He fingered the piece of bone he had purchased from the pseudo-centurion outside the Colosseum. It was formed in the shape of a coin and served as a ticket that the Romans had used to get into the gladiatorial games all those thousands of years ago. The fake centurion assured him that it was a real artifact from ancient Rome, but Bob knew it wasn't. It was probably just a replica. He didn't care. It was still cool. He pulled it out of his pocket and looked at it. He knew in the ancient times there would have been a seat number stamped into the bone to let the visitor know where to sit. This piece had nothing etched on it. It certainly looked like a piece of ancient bone. It didn't feel like some cheap plastic replica. No, he thought. There's no way this is authentic. He rolled it in his fingers and dropped it back into his pocket.

The centurion told him to make a wish and drop it on the arena floor. It was way better than tossing a penny into a fountain, the centurion had said. The wish was way more powerful. The guy had been so serious, too. Bob laughed to himself. It was absolutely ridiculous, but he still wanted to do it.

The tour group stood in a narrow hallway beneath the Colosseum. The guide was a thin Italian man with a narrow face and a big, broad smile. His name was Julius Valentine. Some idiot cracked, "Julius, like orange Julius?" when he had first told them his name, and the tour guide had said back, "I prefer Julius, like Julius Caesar, thank you very much." Bob had smiled at that. He liked this guy. Julius was a great host.

A group of Koreans clutched their smartphones, snapping pictures every two seconds. An Egyptian couple held hands, taking it all in quietly. Several other clusters of Americans completed the tour group. Bob wasn't with any of them. He had been able to break away for the rest of the day from a business symposium he was attending in Rome. He was part of an International Monetary Fund scrutinizing Italian accounts. They were supposed to finalize the plans over how a one-trillion euro fund to rescue beleaguered countries would be funded and operated. But he already knew how he was going to vote on the Italian portion of the measure. He was going to turn it down. And he let everybody know it. The Italians could fight their own way out of their own financial mess. Sure they had a glorious history, but that didn't gave their modern counterparts a free pass for financial stupidity.

"Now you may wonder why these hallways are so narrow," Julius said, continuing his tour talk. "Certainly this looks like a poorly designed piece of work, does it not? So crowded. So confining."

Some heads nodded.

Julius raised his hand. "Ah, but no. It was designed this way on purpose. So the wild animals did not have room to turn around and bite their masters as they were being guided up to the arena floor. Pretty clever of the architects, if you ask me."

Enlightened looks lit up many faces.

"The animal hunts and fights were held in the mornings. Lions, leopards, crocodiles, bulls, bears, panthers, elephants, and many others. Sometimes hunters would be in the arena with them, simulating a hunt in the wild with spears or bows, or even with just daggers and swords for those exceptionally skilled bestiarius. Other times the animals would be pitted against each other."

The tour group moved on and stopped before a row of small rooms.

"Now these tiny rooms were more like holding cells for the prisoners. They were full of convicted criminals waiting their turn to die in the arena. These kinds of brutal executions happened during the midday. Some of these criminals would be burned alive, and some would be prey for starving wild beasts.

Some of them were forced to fight each other to the death. Many of the senators and wealthy patrons of Rome would leave to get lunch during this time. They didn't have as much appetite for this barbarism as the common man, or so the histories tell us."

"Can we go inside them?" someone asked.

"Certainly. You all look like a bunch of criminals to me, anyway," Julius replied.

A few people laughed.

Bob stepped into one of the tiny rooms. One of the stone walls had some kind of etchings carved into it. He couldn't tell if they were letters or just some random grooves. He felt a gaze on him and glanced up to see Julius looking at him.

"Those are a dying man's last words," he said to Bob. Julius motioned with his head to the carvings in the stone wall.

"What does it say?" Bob asked.

"What do most criminals say?" Julius asked.

Bob had no answer.

"I am innocent," Julius said and smiled.

Bob smiled back. "Yeah, right." He looked back at the ancient words.

The tour group moved on. They reached a wider corridor that criss-crossed the narrow corridor they were in, the hallway opening out in a wider area where they could all stand around Julius.

"Please, everyone stand very still and be very quiet," Julius said.

"Why?" someone asked, immediately disobeying the tour guide's request.

Julius raised his hand to his lips. "Please, just for a moment. Quiet and still."

After a few seconds of confused grunts, everyone quieted.

"Sometimes the past speaks to us here," Julius whispered. "Does anyone hear it?"

"Hear what?" someone whispered back.

"The corridors echoing," Julius said. "Sometimes I can hear the officials of the games shouting orders, animals growling and roaring and gnashing their teeth, gladiators testing their weapons. Sometimes even prisoners wailing and moaning as they await their gruesome fate."

"For real?"

Julius nodded. "Yes, sometimes I can. Not always, but sometimes I can hear the sounds from when the Colosseum was at the height of its glory. Sometimes I can hear the slaves working the cages and the ramps."

"The ramps?"

Julius nodded. "Slaves could raise a cage with a leopard, a lion, or some other wild animal inside, into position just below the arena." He pointed out a slot angling down from the top of the wall. "A wooden ramp would go into that slot. Then the animal could climb right from the cage and go straight into the arena," he said.

"I heard something," someone proclaimed. "It sounded like growling." She looked around excitedly. "Did anyone else hear that?"

"That was my stomach," a man said near her. "It's telling me it's almost lunch time."

Some of the tourists laughed.

Julius smiled wanly. "The moment is lost. Let's move on."

The tour guide swept his arm out in front of him. "And this is the arena floor. Where all of the action happened."

Bob stared out at the arena floor.

"Go on," Julius said. "You can step out there. We usually don't put sand out there, but they let us today. It's a special day." Julius smiled.

The tour group moved out into the arena. Bob stood at the threshold, staring down at the sand that covered the arena floor. He took a step and pressed his foot down on the sand. He knew it was just modern sand they probably trucked in from a local home supply store, but the feeling was still amazing. He took a few more steps out into the arena. He was standing on the arena floor of the Colosseum in Rome! Wow. He never thought he'd live to see the day.

"Why sand, some of you may ask," Julius said. "Some of you may know already."

"To soak up all the blood," someone said.

Julius nodded. "Yes. There was plenty of blood when the games were held. Animal blood and human blood. The sand soaked it up and the arena workers could quickly rake it away and apply a fresh layer between events."

Bob fingered the bone ticket in his pocket. Ridiculous. Childish. But stupidly fun. He took the ticket out of his pocket, hiding it in his curled up fingers. He glanced around at the others, casting them surreptitious glances, but no one was paying any attention to him.

He made a wish and dropped the bone ticket into the sand.

What Bob didn't see was Julius the tour guide watching him out of the corner of his vision. What he didn't hear was Julius utter a wish of his own before the ticket hit the sand. What Bob didn't understand was what happened next because he hadn't wished for it. He hadn't wished for it at all.

And the next thing Bob knew he was still standing on the arena floor. But the noise was deafening. He looked up to see thousands of faces staring at him from all directions. Many of the front rows of marble seats were empty, but there were still enough bodies filling the rest of the Colosseum to create a thunderous wave of sound. It was such a jumble of discordant noise Bob didn't know if people were cheering or jeering.

This isn't what I wished for, was the first thought that came to Bob's mind. I'm supposed to be surrounded by beautiful Roman woman in scanty clothes. They're supposed to be dancing for me, and feeding me grapes, and pleasuring me. Then the weirdness of the situation struck him. Wait a minute, where is the tour group? Bob frowned. He glanced quickly around him, but the tour group was not visible anywhere near him. What the hell? Where did all the other people in the tour group go? He looked back up at the throngs of people in the seats that surround the arena floor. Where the hell had they all come from?

And then a strong smell suddenly hit him. A biting

smell of blood and sweat and death. Bob hadn't smelled much death in his life but he somehow immediately knew what the stench was that assailed his nose. It was most certainly the reeking stench of death.

A sword hit the ground at Bob's feet, splashing sand onto his bare feet. Why are my feet bare? he wondered. Then he noticed his ankles were exposed, and his shins, and his thighs. I'm naked, Bob realized with absolute stark terror. I'm fucking naked. What the hell? Where is that damned tour guide? I've got to be dreaming. He had dreams of being naked on stage in front of a group of men and women in professional business attire before, but nothing that felt as real as this dream did.

A savage guttural cry coming from behind Bob made him turn in time to see a naked wild man charging at him, his hands curved into claws, the man's eyes wide and filled with madness. Blood streaked the man's face, his bare chest, his arms, his legs. Bob ducked without thinking and the man sailed over him; Bob could feel the man's penis dragging across his back as the man skidded over him. It felt so real. It was the most vivid dreamed he had ever had in his entire life. This is not a dream, Bob thought with a disturbing sense of dread. He instinctively snatched at the sword in the sand at his feet and gripped it tightly, turning to the wild man.

The wild man was already back on his feet, charging at him again. Bob hacked at him, hitting the wild man in the shoulder, sinking the sharp blade into the man's flesh. Blood sprayed up from the gouge, hitting Bob in the chest and neck. Some of the red spray splattered against his cheek.

The wild man shrieked an awful scream, clutching at the sword buried in his flesh. Bob yanked the blade out of the wild man's shoulder. The wild man just dropped to the sand and flopped about grotesquely, screaming and slapping at the deep wound as if that would stop the massive flow of blood streaming out from his shoulder.

Bob stared at the dying man. After another few moments of spasmodic motions, the man was still. The man's eyes faced upwards, open, empty, and lifeless. The sand absorbed his blood in dark blotches. This is not what I wished for, Bob thought.

The sound of the roaring crowd completely engulfed him. Bob looked up to see all the faces staring at him, shouting, laughing, jeering, leering, smiling. Not one face was still. They were all full of emotion of one sort or the other, all intently watching him.

Bob looked at all the empty marble seats in the front rows. These seats were positioned just behind the large wall that surrounded the arena. Why were they so empty when the rest of the arena was so jammed full of people? Something nagged at him about that.

Bob glanced down at the blood-streaked sword in his hand. What the hell was happening? It all had happened so fast. My God, he had just killed a man. He had just slain someone in the arena. He had a sudden compulsion to relish his victory. He raised his sword up, pointing the bloody tip high into the air. What a great dream! But there was a voice inside him that continued to whisper an urgent warning at him. This is not a dream.

The applause was so thunderous it felt like it

shook the entire Colosseum. Bob felt himself growing stronger the louder the applause grew. He turned round and round, basking in the crowd's roar, absorbing the cheering into himself as if he were absorbing the sun's rays. If this was a dream, he was going for it! He would play it out to the end. Maybe he would win the famous wooden sword of freedom. He could buy a villa. And surround himself with women in sexy stolas! Oh, yes, all those delicious women pleasuring him with decadent Roman sex games. This is not a dream. The warning went ignored.

Bob looked again at the empty lower seats. He knew those marble seats were usually filled by senators and other important men of Rome, but they were mostly vacant now. And then he realized why. It must be the noon hour. The hour when criminals were executed. The prominent members of Rome usually left during these barbaric displays of justice. Julius told them that. But I'm not a criminal, Bob thought. He glanced around the arena again. Where the hell was that tour guide? His thoughts were a jumbled mess of the present and what was happening to him in his dream. This is not a dream, the warning voice repeated yet again.

Bob saw movement out of the corner of his eye and spun to see a gladiator charging up onto the arena floor from a newly opened ramp. Bob knew what type of gladiator this man was. He had seen numerous pictures of his type in history books and had seen his type in a few movies. The man was a retiarius. The gladiator was dressed in a loincloth held in place by a wide belt. He had a metal forearm guard and shoulder guard on his left arm. The man clutched a three-pointed trident in his left hand and a weighted net in his right. The trident was about six feet in length, its tips razor sharp. The net was laced with hard balls at various spots along the net to give it weight. Bob knew the retiarius used the net to try and trap his opponent beneath it, or tangle his opponent's weapon up in it and make it ineffective. If the retiarius managed to trap an opponent in his net, then the gladiator could easily deliver a killing strike with the long reach of his trident.

Bob lowered his sword and moved to a crouched position. The retiarius whirled the net at him, but Bob ducked away, avoiding the attack. The retiarius thrust his trident forward and Bob barely managed to avoid getting struck. Bob thrust his sword down and the blade deflected the spear. One of the outer tips of the trident grazed Bob's leg, but it didn't break his skin. He swung his sword at the retiarius, but the gladiator easily dodged his strike.

The retiarius reached the thrown net and gathered it back up in his right hand. The gladiator circled him, thrusting the trident forward at Bob's bare feet. Bob danced away from the stabbing prongs. All around him, he could hear the audience laughing. The gladiator was toying with him. The retiarius was making him dance for the crowd. Bob grit his teeth and his jaw tightened. He re-gripped his sword.

The retiarius continued to circle him and jab the trident at his feet. Bob backed away quickly, moving away from the sharp tips. Then Bob saw the gladiator tighten up his right hand. It was a tell. He knew the man was getting ready to throw the net again. Instead of ducking away, Bob dove forward, hitting the sand on his shoulder as the net sailed over him. He rolled up, thrusting his sword sharply forward as he came out of the shoulder roll. The sword went in deep into the retiarius's exposed stomach. Blood seeped out from around the edges of the sword, staining the retiarius's skin red. Bob pushed the blade in deeper. The gladiator gurgled and lost his grip on the trident, the long weapon falling to the arena sand. Bob withdrew his sword from the man's body and more blood spilled forth. The gladiator keeled over to hit the sand with a dull thud. The sand absorbed the stream of blood oozing out from the gash in the retiarius's gut.

The arena went silent.

But only for a moment. Then the cheers and shouts and stomping and clapping resumed at a mighty roar. Bob again raised his blood-streaked sword. He thrust it high. Blood ran down the blade, over the handle, and down his fingers. The sounds of the crowd buffeted him like a gale wind and he absorbed it all. He could do it. He could beat these savage bastards in their own game. As he glanced at the death and carnage and pools of red splashed everywhere, he realized with a sickening sensation gnawing at the pit of his stomach that he had gotten his wish after all. It wasn't a wish full of busty Roman babes in stolas feeding him grapes and pleasuring him in all manners of perverse ways. But he did get his Roman orgy. A Roman orgy of blood.

That's when the trap door sprung open behind him and the two black panthers came leaping out onto the sand.

Bob didn't even have to time to publicly profess his innocence.

"Time to move on," Julius said, ushering the tour group off the arena floor. No one even noticed that the group was one member short.

Behind them on the arena floor, a red stain spread through the sand.

.

TERRORSTORY #19
FLIPBOOK

"**W**hat the hell is wrong with you?"

I squinted dumbly at my wife. "What?" I hadn't even made it through the screen door and she was already on me.

Lindsey thrust the tiny book at me as I walked through the front door. "Didn't you even look at this before you gave it to her?" She still had a sheen of perspiration on her face from exercising. Her blonde hair was plastered to the side of her face, slick with sweat. Her cheeks were a bright red. She was into some kind of yoga aerobics that really gave her a good workout. At least this week she was. Next week it would probably be back to couch surfing with a bottle in her hand. Her cheeks would still be the same red, but it wouldn't be from any vigorous exercise.

I glanced down at the book in her hand. I had just gotten chewed out by Haster for not finding a new printing partner in China we could outsource some of our printing jobs to, so I really wasn't in the mood for her ragging at me, too. "It's just a flipbook."

Lindsey thrust the little book at me again. "I know it's a flipbook. Did you even look at it?"

"Yeah, I looked at it."

"Really? And you *still* gave it to her? Are you a damned idiot?"

I frowned and took the book from her and read the title again. *Flippin' Fun and Games.* That was harmless. I flipped through the book, thumbing through the pages quickly so the little animated cartoon scene played out as the pages fluttered past. What I saw was disgusting. My frown deepened. I looked up at my wife. "This is not what I saw. It was just a cute little scene with a dog. It looked just like Danielle playing fetch with Crusty like she always does."

"That doesn't look like a cute scene to me."

I flipped through the pages again. The frown remained. I felt my stomach churn. "Lindsey, I swear that wasn't what I saw."

"You really need to get your head out of your ass, George. You should be ashamed of yourself for giving her something like that." She looked at me with that disgusted look I had seen far too often. "Really, what the hell is wrong with you?" Lindsey turned and walked away before I had a chance to defend myself. "I have to go pick up Danielle from play practice at the high school." She snatched her keys off the kitchen island and stormed out.

I flipped through the pages again. The tiny cartoon revealed a dog getting run over by a pickup truck. It was awful. The dog was flattened beneath the big oversized wheels of the truck. I flipped through the images again. Jesus, this is not possible, I thought. This is not the picture I saw when I flipped through the book at the flea market. How the hell could it change? I turned the little book over in my hands, looking for some kind of electronic device, a chip, a battery port, something. It had to be some kind of newfangled gizmo or something. Some kind of new smartbook or something. But I didn't see anything out the ordinary. It just looked like a dog-eared flipbook that was dozens of years old. I tossed the book into a nearby waste basket.

That's when a horrifying thud and shrill whimpering shriek rang out from the front yard.

"You ever heard of a digital flipbook?"

I looked at my neighbor Vince with squinted eyes. He was a swarthy Cuban with just a touch of hair left on his nearly-bald head. We sat outside in lawn chairs on his driveway, drinking beer. Vince had his feet propped up on the scratched and battered cooler that he always pulled out for our bullshit sessions. He was a good guy, a good neighbor to shoot the shit with. He had a grueling job with heavy driving in rush hour traffic every day, so his favorite thing to do when he finally got home was to crack open a cold one and relax for a few minutes. I often joined him. We both had enough work horror stories to fill up a few seasons of a reality TV show. But today I didn't want to talk about work. I had to tell somebody about that damned book.

"You know, those books where you flip the pages really fast and some little cartoon thingy plays," I explained. "Right? You know what I'm talking about."

"Yeah, but I never heard of a digital flipbook. How the heck do you flip digital pages? Don't it need to be paper or something?"

"Man, I don't know. But it's gotta be digital or something."

"Why?" Vince asked.

"Because the cartoon changes."

"Yeah, so? That's stupid."

"It ain't stupid." I paused. "You wanna know why it ain't stupid?"

Vince said nothing.

"I'll tell you why? Because the shit I saw in the cartoon happened. You know when Danielle's dog got hit yesterday?" I still heard the yelp ringing in my mind. I did my best to push the memory of the sound away, but it still lingered in the back of my head.

Vince nodded. "Yeah, sure sorry to hear about that. Crusty was a damn good dog." He tipped his bottle forward in salute, then took a drink of his beer. It was some Polish brew he had just discovered at Binny's. He was always discovering new beers. Gave him a great excuse to keep drinking them.

"Yeah, well, I saw that," I told him. "Last time I flipped the pages, I fucking saw that. I saw him getting hit by that truck." The yelp echoed in my thoughts. I raised the flipbook and waved it in front of Vince, hoping that might wave the awful sound away from inside my head, too, but it didn't; I could still hear Crusty's yelp echoing through my head over and over and over. "I saw it in here. I saw Crusty getting hit."

Vince frowned at me.

"But when I flipped through the book the first time I found it, I just saw a cute little cartoon of a dog playing. It looked just like Crusty, so that's why I got it for Danielle."

Vince was quiet for a long moment. He took another drink from his beer. "Where'd you get it?"

"That flea market in Karlin County. The one on Raindall Road."

"You ever see any lottery numbers on that thing?" Vince took another swig of beer.

"No, it ain't like that. It shows me stuff. Things happening. You know, like… incidents."

"Incidents?"

"Yeah, shit that happens."

Vince nodded, but I could tell he wasn't believing me. "Let me try it."

He reached for the flipbook and I quickly yanked it away from him. I didn't want him to touch it. Ever since I pulled it back out of the garbage, I felt an intense need to keep the book on me at all times. The thought of someone else even handling the flipbook made me feel real angry. I don't know why; it just did. I should have let him take it. Maybe that would have stopped… But I didn't. And now I'm paying for it.

"Show me," Vince said. "What's the cartoon now? Did it change?"

I did need to show him. "Yeah, it changed." I needed to show somebody. I needed to know that I wasn't going crazy. "Okay," I said. I grabbed the book and put my thumb up on the cover, getting set to flip the pages. "You ready?"

"Man, just flip the damn pages."

I flipped the pages. And we watched the scene, the incident, unfold on the pages as they flipped by. When I reached the end of the pages, I just held the flipbook in my hand.

"You need to show me that again," Vince said.

I showed him again, flipping through the pages. The animated scene played out. We were both pretty damn quiet for a long time.

"Are you kidding me?" Vince finally said. "You think *that* is going to happen? There's no way."

Oh, how wrong he was.

"You watching the news?" I held my phone to my ear, talking to Vince.

"Yeah, but I'm not believing it."

"I told you."

He was real quiet.

"You there, man?" I asked.

"What if we caused it?" Vince said.

"What?"

"What if we caused it? What if we made it happen?"

"How could we have caused a fire to burn down Wrigley Field?"

He was real quiet again.

"Vince?"

"Yeah." He paused. "We should have told somebody. We should have warned somebody. *You* should have called somebody. You should have told somebody, man. Anybody."

"Me?"

"You knew it was going to happen. I didn't believe you," Vince said. "Now I believe you. But you knew that was going to happen, didn't you? I mean, you really knew, right?"

I didn't have an answer to that. Did I really think it would happen? At the time, I'm not sure. It just seemed too outrageous. Just downright impossible. But he was right. I should have warned somebody. I should have called in some kind of anonymous tip or something. I should have done a lot of things differently before...

"That damned flipbook of yours. It's cursed. You should shred it," Vince said and hung up on me.

He was right. I should have shredded it. Right then and there. I should have destroyed it. I should have burned it. But I didn't. I couldn't after what I had just seen. I just couldn't. Not after the new animation revealed itself.

I grabbed the flipbook and angrily flipped through it again and again. But the cartoon never changed. I knew why. I knew why it wouldn't change. Because it hadn't happened yet. The ugly scene had not played out yet in real life.

The scene with my wife and my daughter.

I flipped through the pages again. Yeah, Lindsey was drinking a lot again and her and Danielle could get into some nasty fights, but that was just how those two were. They knew how to push each other's buttons. But they always made up after they fought.

I flipped through the pages again and felt sweat lining my brow. Maybe this time they wouldn't make up. Maybe this time it would get really ugly. Otherwise why would Lindsey stab Danielle with a butcher knife?

I should have just showed Lindsey the flipbook. But I didn't. Instead, I watched her. Did I want to see what I saw in those tiny pages come to fruition? Did I want it to happen? No! That's a horrible, terrible thought. I didn't want it to happen. *Why not? Then you would be free of them both.* No, I didn't want it to happen!

I watched Lindsey out of the corner of my eye, always keeping her in sight whenever she was around, gauging her mood, guessing at her mental status from across the room. I found some empty wine bottles shoved down into the kitchen garbage can, so I knew she was drinking every night again now. I tried to stay out of her way, just so anything I did wouldn't set her off.

I should have warned Danielle. I should have just showed her the flipbook. But I didn't. I don't know why. Maybe I just didn't want to believe it. I knew she already blamed me for Crusty's death. It wasn't logical. It wasn't fair, but she did. I had nothing to do with our dog's death, but she just joined the two together in her head, me showing her the flipbook and Crusty dying soon after. She already looked at me with disgust every time I came near her. I didn't want that look to get any darker, any uglier than it already was. So I didn't tell her.

I just watched them both. Every time they were near each other the muscles in my neck squeezed tight until my head felt like it was going to pop off from the pressure.

Every so often, I flipped through the pages again. The scene did not change.

Lindsey waved the carving knife at Danielle. "One of these days, Danielle. One of these days."

My heart nearly leapt out of my throat. I reached up to grab her arm, but Lindsey pulled the knife back down and I dropped my hand. Jesus. It was the most stressful pumpkin carving day I ever had. Every time Lindsey shoved the knife into the pumpkin, the thick meaty sound made my stomach turn. She tried to cut a straight mouth, but her inebriated brain carved out a jagged crooked line.

Danielle worked on her pumpkin, reaching her hand in to scoop out the seeds and stringy insides of the big orange gourd. "Everybody's going, Mom. So I'm going." She used her prissy entitled voice, the one she just knew pissed Lindsey off. She had sixteen years to practice and she was damned good at riling up her mother.

"What are you, a sheep? A lemming?" Lindsey asked her in a snippy tone.

Danielle paused and cocked her head sharply. She pushed her blonde hair away from her eyes with the back of her hand. "What the hell is a lemming?"

"It's one of those little animals who just follow each other over a cliff," Lindsey said. "Is that what you are? Just a follower?"

"Shut up, Mom." Danielle continued to scoop the guts out of her pumpkin and plop them on the newspapers that covered the kitchen table.

"Don't tell me to shut up."

"I am not missing that party." Danielle shook her head. "No way."

Lindsey turned her red-streaked eyes to me. "You gonna chime in? No, of course you're not." She turned away from me to look back at Danielle. "And how are you going to get there?"

"Billy is gonna pick me up, ha!"

"That son of a bitch is driving now? Heaven help us all." Lindsey stabbed the knife into the pumpkin. "You gonna blow him for his troubles?"

"Lindsey, really, is that necessary?" I asked. I kept my voice calm. She ignored me.

"I think *you* just want to blow him," Danielle retorted.

And so it went on.

Lindsey's pumpkin stared at me with a drunk, amused grin.

Two days later, it happened.

I heard a chilling scream and charged into Danielle's bedroom. There stood Lindsey, a grotesque mask covering her face, a butcher knife in her hand, raised high and ready to strike.

I didn't think. I just kept going right at her. I hit Lindsey hard in the mid-section and she teetered towards the open window. She hit the window ledge, and her body distorted, her waist section extending out the window. The knife dropped out of her hand as she clutched at the edges of the window frame, but the momentum kept her body going. Her fingers scraped at the wall as she fell out the window. She screamed on the way down. I heard a sickening thud, then there was no sound from outside.

Danielle screamed. "Daddy! What are you doing?" She raced to the window. She looked down and screamed. She whirled on me. "What did you do?"

"I— She was attacking you. She was going to— kill you."

"We were rehearsing my play! It was just my play!" Danielle sobbed and dropped to the floor, tears streaming down her face. "What did you do?"

I flipped the pages. The pictures had changed. The tiny cartoon was a cute little animated snippet of a man being taken away in handcuffs by uniformed police officers. The man was me. They were coming to take me away.

I'm in my prison cell now. Sometimes they take the white jacket off me, sometimes they don't. Guess it depends on their mood. They don't let any other prisoners in with me. They think I'm contagious or something. Well, fuck them. The truth *should* be contagious. Fucking assholes won't listen to reason.

The flipbook is with me. I keep it hidden in a hole beneath one of the loose legs of the bed and they haven't found it yet. Somebody sent it to me in the mail. Who, I don't know. Somebody's idea of a sick joke, perhaps. I'm afraid it might have been my daughter. She hasn't spoken to me since — that horrible day. Hell, maybe it was Vince. He thinks this is all my fault. It could have been Lindsey's sister. She wants me to get the electric chair and she even volunteered to throw the switch. Who knows? They all think I'm insane anyway.

My hand shakes every time I look at the flipbook. I don't even have to touch it. I just have to think about touching it and my fingers tremble. I do wonder if I caused everything. Maybe if I hadn't flipped the pages, the book would have just retained the same little cartoon graphic. Maybe because I did flip the pages I caused those things to happen. Maybe it was all because of me. Maybe all those horrible things happened because of me. All because I couldn't stop myself from flipping the pages.

I have to look again. I have to watch it. I have to flip the pages. I grab the book and I flip the pages again, letting the thin pieces of paper glide along my fingers. The animation plays out for the millionth time. I can't turn my gaze from it. I have to watch it. Can such a thing really happen?

I flip the pages again. The animated pictures do not change.

I flip the pages again. The pictures do not change.

I flip the pages again. No change.

I know it will change. If I keep flipping the pages, it will change. The animation has to change. It must! I will keep flipping the pages until it does! It will change!

I should warn everyone. I should tell Vince. I should tell Danielle. But no one will believe me. Even my daughter won't believe me. I'm locked up in a prison cell for the murder of her mother. Oh my God. I killed Lindsey. Sometimes it hits me like a sledgehammer and I cry for hours. Other times, I just feel numb and my eyes stay dry.

I flip the pages again. The pictures do not change. I tried to tell people about the book, but every time I did they just looked at me with the same '*you are mad*' look that they always gave me.

I should show the warden. I should show him the book. But then they would take it away from me. I hate the book with every fiber of my being, but I can't let it go. I hate the thought of someone else possessing it even more. It needs to stay with me.

I flip the pages again. I still can't tell what city it is. Maybe Chicago. Maybe New York. Maybe Dallas or Nashville. I just don't know for sure. Regardless of what city it is, the mushroom cloud still billows up into the air. Who do I tell? Who will believe me?

I flip the pages again. The pictures do not change.

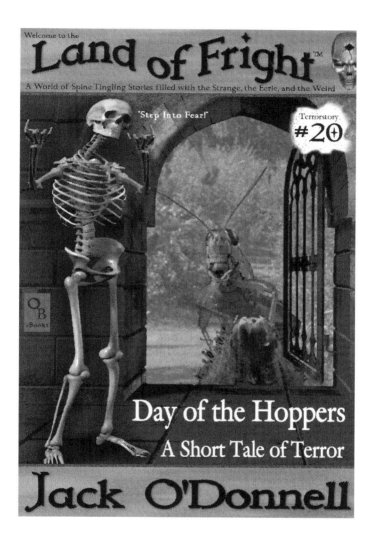

TERRORSTORY #20
DAY OF THE HOPPERS

If Greg Littles had known what the tingling beneath his feet had really meant, he would have started running right away. But he didn't. So he stayed where he was. Besides, he had a backyard to defend. He shifted his grip on the cool metal handle of the garbage can lid, holding his makeshift shield before him. He re-gripped the plastic yellow wiffle ball bat and held it at his side. He peered through a vertical slat in the fence, scanning Roger's backyard.

"Did you finish your homework?" his mother shouted from the back stoop.

Greg looked over to see her standing in the open screen doorway. "Yeah, mom," he yelled back. The lie came naturally with no effort. He wasn't finished. He hadn't even started the paper he had to write. Mr. Bloomquist, his current events teacher, wanted everyone to write a paper on thundering. Some thundering company had set up shop half a dozen miles from town in some old abandoned cornfields. Greg didn't know a lot about thundering, but he knew they were looking to extract oil or natural gas or stuff like that. It was like fracking, but supposedly a lot safer for the environment because they used sound waves instead of pressurized fluid. Something about sending sonic booms deep into the earth to shake rocks loose so more gas could flow. It was all everyone seemed to be talking about lately, so Greg picked up bits and pieces just by listening to his parents talk on the phone, in the store, at the diner; wherever they went thundering seemed to be the only topic of conversation. But mostly everyone was talking about how thundering could make everybody who owned even the smallest parcel of land in town rich, just like fracking had done for a lot of people.

Something exploded on a fence slat several rows away from him. *He got behind me!* Greg spun, looking for his friend. *What's he doing? Throwing rocks at me?* He raised his garbage can lid shield. Wham! Something struck the center of the lid with the force of a fastball, knocking him back into the fence. Greg grimaced at the pain in his knuckles as the force of the blow knocked the metal of his garbage can lid shield into his fingers. He tilted the lid to look at it and saw a red smear splattering the gray metal. *What the hell? He's shooting paintballs at me.* But then he looked closer at the red streak and saw some odd fragments of green and black. Was that an insect's leg?

Splaat! Craack! Two more sharp explosions rang out. Greg looked at the fence to his left, seeing two more bright red smears marring the white pickets. A whistling sound grew louder and he instinctively raised his shield towards his head. Another projectile struck the shield on the upper edge of the lid, jarring it loose from his grip.

"Greg." That was Roger, calling to him from Roger's backyard.

Greg clutched at the fallen shield, raising it back up to protect his body. More projectiles whistled past his head. He felt one brush against his pant leg, just barely missing him. He heard multiple splatters against the fence behind him.

"Greg!"

He turned toward the sound of his friend's urgent voice. He saw Roger huddled in his yard next door, crouched down behind several large potted plants. Red splatters dotted the area all around him. "Over here!" Greg shouted to him.

"Something hit me in the head! I got blood in my eyes!"

Greg could hear the terror in Roger's voice. "Stay there. I'm coming over." Greg raced to the back corner of his yard. He moved over to the fence and pushed several loose slats out of the way, nudging them aside with his shoulder. It was a secret passageway he and Roger had discovered last summer; it connected their backyards. He tossed his wiffle ball bat down, but kept his garbage can lid shield.

He raced over to Roger and huddled down next to him behind the pots. Roger was twelve just like he was, their birthdays only a few weeks apart. They both were also left-handed and had picked up the nicknames Lefty Lemon and Lefty Lime. Neither one could remember who was supposed to be who, but they didn't care; they both responded to either one if someone used them in conversation. A stone wall protected their backs from the flying projectiles Greg could hear coming from the opposite direction. Whatever the projectiles were, they hit the wall with dull thuds on the other side of the stones.

"What's going on?" Roger asked.

Greg shook his head. "I don't know."

"I think it's the grasshoppers," Roger said, answering his own question.

"What?"

"It's the grasshoppers. They're going crazy." Roger pointed to several dead grasshoppers laying on the ground nearby. Their bodies were mangled and smashed. "I saw them jump straight into the pots. They're going kamikaze."

"What?"

"Like those Japanese pilots. The ones that dive-bombed ships during World War Two. We just learned about them in history. Jeez, don't you ever pay attention in class?" Roger gently tapped at his forehead. "One of them cut my head."

Greg looked up to see the red smear across Roger's forehead. "It's still bleeding."

Roger wiped at the blood. "I know."

"We need to get into the house." A weird tingling feeling surged in Greg's legs. He could feel it in his knees where they were touching the ground. "Do you feel that?"

Roger looked to him.

"That tingling. In your legs?"

Roger nodded. "I felt it right before everything started going crazy."

"Me, too."

"What is it?" Roger asked.

Greg shook his head. "I don't know. Some kind of earthquake or something, maybe."

Roger shook his head. "That's not an earthquake. I felt tons of earthquakes when I lived in California. None of them ever felt like this."

A pot shattered next to them and they looked in nervous awe at the shattered grasshopper bodies that dotted the ground near it.

"You ready to make a run for it?" Greg asked. He clutched at his garbage can lid shield.

Roger lifted his garbage can lid shield and nodded. "Okay, go!"

Greg bolted upright, but found himself soaring through the air, rocketing towards the plate glass window of Roger's back porch door at an alarming speed. He raised the garbage can lid in front him and exploded through the window in an eruption of glass.

Roger hit the living room floor right next to him, both of them rolling and tumbling along the carpeting until the couch stopped their movement. Shards of glass littered the carpet all around them. They both fought to catch their breaths, then scrambled around to the other side of the couch, using it as a protective wall.

"What just happened?" Roger asked, his words coming out in quick panting grunts.

"I don't know. I just started going towards the house, then I just leaped through the air."

Roger nodded. "It felt like my legs were like giant springs or something. I just jumped after you and then I was flying through the air."

"This is crazy," Greg muttered.

A loud explosion rang out from the front of the house.

They raced to the front window to see a car on fire just half a block down.

"Is that a body? Holy crap. Greg, is that some lady's body in the street?" Roger asked.

Greg ignored his question. He glanced around the living room. "Are your parents home?"

Roger shook his head. He pulled his gaze away from the window, away from the chaos outside. "No, they're in New York on business. My aunt is supposed to come and stay with me tonight." Roger looked at Greg. "What the heck is going on, Greg?"

"Let's go to my house. I know my mom and dad are home."

Roger nodded.

Greg sat with Roger at their kitchen table, watching his dad Barry pace the kitchen floor. Greg's mom Jill had cleaned out Roger's cut and bandaged his forehead. Amazingly, their explosive entry into Roger's house hadn't even left any additional scratches on either one of them. They had already told Greg's dad what had happened in the backyard with the grasshoppers going berserk.

All around them, they could hear tiny popping sounds as insect projectiles struck the house. Occasionally, a much louder bang sounded out. *They are trying to get in. They're trying to reach us*, Greg thought.

Barry Littles paced for a long time, rubbing at his forehead with his thumb and forefinger, talking to himself, obviously mentally churning through the events happening outside, trying to find some rationale for the disturbing activity. He suddenly stopped and whirled to face Jill. "It's like flowback, but with sound," Barry said. He resumed his pacing, continuing to rub at his forehead with his thumb and forefinger, repeating what he had just said softly to himself. "What else could it be?" he muttered. "I told them something like this could happen. It wasn't thoroughly tested." He shook his head. "But nobody listens to the naysayers."

"What the hell are you talking about, Barry?"

Barry stopped and turned to Jill. "Damn it, Jill, flowback! You know. When the liquid they use in fracking returns back up to the surface. It's like that, but they aren't using liquid in thundering. They're using high pressure sound waves for thundering." He resumed pacing.

Jill frowned at Barry.

Barry stopped and turned back to her again. "Jesus, Jill. The sound. The sound waves. The earth is pushing them back at us. It's turning them into energy and pushing them back at us."

"That's crazy."

Barry pointed outside. "And that isn't?"

Jill shook her head.

"It's passing kinetic energy into insects somehow." Barry looked at Greg and Roger. "Maybe into people even."

Jill continued to shake her head. "That's not possible."

"It's possible! It's happening!" Barry rubbed his fingers through his sparse hair. He paced back and forth, then stopped to face Jill. "It's like in a pool game when you slam the cue ball into another ball and the cue ball stops dead, but the other ball picks up the kinetic energy and goes careening off. The earth is generating hundreds of elastic collisions. Transferring the energy into the grasshoppers that attacked the boys." He paused. "Millions of collisions. Jesus, maybe billions." Barry paused for a long moment, his hand still on his head. "My God... *trillions.*"

The insect projectiles hit the car side panels with loud pings. Greg thought it sounded like someone was throwing rocks at them. He was scrunched down in the back seat of their car. Roger was scrunched down next to him; his aunt had never shown up. Barry didn't want to leave any of them alone in the house, so he made them come with him. Both Greg and Roger had their garbage can lid shields; it made them both feel safer to have their makeshift shields with them.

They had tried to call the police department, but they could not get through. The road leading to the police station was impassable with half a dozen overturned cars and two burning vehicles blocking the road. Barry made a snap decision when he saw the traffic jam and turned up Norton Street. They headed up the road that led to the big thundering machine that was erected outside of town.

They had no plan. It just seemed like the logical

place to go since they couldn't reach the police station or the fire department. Barry wanted to see if the facility was still operating, see if the thundering machine was somehow really the cause of all this craziness.

<hr/>

They sat in the car, staring out the front window. Bloodied bodies lay strewn about the thundering site. They didn't see anyone moving. Not anyone human. The air was still filled with a flurry of movement everywhere they looked. Insects exploded against the car doors, the windows.

"Jesus, are they all dead?" Jill asked.

No one answered.

They just stared.

The huge thundering machine was still active. They could feel the ground shaking as it sent one sonic wave after the other deep into the earth. It was a subtle feeling of movement because the sound waves were being released far below the surface, but they could still feel it all the same.

"Do you really think that is causing it, Dad?" Greg asked.

Barry sat quietly, staring at the big machine. "I don't know what to think."

"How do we shut it off?" Jill asked.

No one had the answer to that question either.

"There's gotta be a switch, right?" Greg asked.

"That would be nice," Barry said. "But I doubt it has a big On/Off switch."

Greg caught movement near the huge machine. "Look! There's a guy over there. He's still alive!

Maybe he can shut it off."

They all watched the man stagger to his feet. He was dressed in heavy work boots and jeans, a white button shirt. But then the man did a spasmodic dance as his body was barraged with a bevy of grasshopper bullets. The insects burst through his chest, through his back, through his belly, through his neck. Dozens of red splotches appeared on his shirt. Crimson stains darkened his jeans. Greg heard his mom whimper in fear as she watched the horrible scene unfold. Greg knew the man was dead long before his body finally collapsed to the cement ground around the machine.

More pinging sounds rang out inside the car as more insects hurtled themselves like kamikazes against the metal body of the vehicle. Kamikazes. Greg did remember learning about them in history class. Japanese Zero pilots who flew their planes straight into aircraft carriers. Kamikazes. Just like Roger had said. Greg looked at the open expanse that was between their car and the machine. "Dad, how do we even reach it?"

"I'm going to move closer," Barry said. He shifted the car into drive. The car slowly moved closer to the thundering machine.

Greg could see the solar panels that helped power the machine situated high atop it. Something troubled him about the huge panels, but he couldn't quite figure out what was bothering him. Their smooth silver surfaces glistened in the hot sun. Then he realized they were untouched. They were still in perfect condition. The insects weren't striking them. They weren't just jumping in wild disorganized patterns. They were aiming. Aiming at them.

The car moved slowly closer to the thundering

machine.

The earth started to shake. Loudly. Violently. The ground shifted, then started to rise up in front of them.

"It's an earthquake!" Jill shrieked. "Stop the car! Barry, stop the car!"

But it wasn't an earthquake. It wasn't an earthquake at all. Huge columns of solid rock rose up in front of them, forming a thick wall of stone between their car and the machine.

They stared at the impassable barrier. For a brief moment, the tall columns of stones blocking their way reminded Greg of huge tombstones.

⚔⚔⚔

"I have an idea," Roger said.

They waited for Roger to continue.

"Greg, remember when we were at the house and this crazy shit started to happen?" Roger stopped and looked at Greg's parents. "Crazy stuff."

"Roger, if you feel like cursing your fucking head off, now is the fucking time to do it," Jill said.

Roger didn't respond to her. He looked back to Greg. "Remember we felt that weird tingling in our feet and our legs?"

Greg nodded. "Yeah. Like we had springs in our legs."

Roger nodded. "Or stored up kinetic energy, like what your dad said earlier." Roger looked over at Barry. "We both were standing still on the ground, getting ready to run to my house, then all of a sudden we jumped super fast and super far."

Greg nodded. "Yeah, yeah." He looked at his dad.

"We told you that. We busted right through his patio window."

Barry nodded. He waited for Roger to continue.

"So what if we did the same thing here?" Roger said. "What if we stand outside and let the energy build up in our legs?"

"And then do what?" Barry asked.

Roger pointed out the car window. "Jump over that."

They followed his pointing finger to stare at the large columns of stones.

"Who's gonna do it?" Greg asked.

"I will," Roger answered immediately.

"And then what?" Barry asked.

"I know how to turn it off," Roger said. "There's a power conduit with an emergency kill switch in the panel. I know where that is. I just remembered it from the field trip we took."

Greg smiled at his friend. "Man, I really gotta pay more attention when I'm at school."

Roger patted Greg on the shoulder. "Yeah, you do."

<hr />

The passenger side rear window was open just a crack so Greg could hear Roger and talk to him, even though he couldn't see his friend. Roger was crouched down in front of the car, using the vehicle as a shield as best he could while the energy built up in his legs. Some big insects exploded hard against the window near Greg's head, cracking the glass. Greg did his best not to shout in alarm, biting back the sound that wanted to burst from his lips. He moved down lower in his seat.

"I'm gonna go," Greg heard Roger say. "My legs are shaking like crazy."

"You got your shield?" Greg asked.

"Yeah."

"Do it, Roger," Greg said. "Go kick some ass, Lefty Lemon."

"I will." There was a pause, then Roger said, "I'm Lefty Lime. You're Lefty Lemon." And then Roger shot upwards into the air, bursting out from his crouched position in front of the right headlight, his garbage can lid shield clutched in front of him. His body sailed high, racing towards the top of the stone wall.

"That's gonna hurt when he lands," Barry said.

Oh, no. Greg felt a moment of panic for his friend. They hadn't even thought about that. They were just completely focused on getting over that wall. They hadn't thought about the hard landing Roger was going to take on the other side of the wall when he came down.

Roger reached the top of the wall of stones and his body kept going, reaching the apex of his jump a few feet above the columns of rock. That's when they struck. Roger's body jerked and twisted and flopped as sprays of blood erupted from him like tiny geysers going off. His garbage can lid shield offered little protection from the massive onslaught. More insect projectiles blasted into him, grotesquely keeping Roger's body aloft for a few more horrible seconds. And then he plummeted back towards the earth, hitting the car's hood with a sickening crack.

Roger's wide eyes stared at Greg. The lefty brothers would never argue over their nicknames again. The garbage can lid shield came crashing down onto Roger's face, smashing his cheek.

Jill whimpered, curling herself into a ball in the front seat.

"Doesn't the earth know we're trying to help it?" Greg asked. He fought back the tears that bit at the corners of his eyes. He turned and pounded on the cracked window glass next to him. "We're trying to help you!"

Barry laughed a bitter laugh. "At this point, I don't think it cares." Then Barry started in his seat, gripping the steering wheel viciously with both hands. "It doesn't want the machine off," he said. "It wants it to stay on! It wants that fucking machine to stay on." Barry put his hand to his head and stared out the window. "It's fighting back," he muttered. "It's finally fighting back."

"What do we do?" Greg asked. "What do we do?"

"We die, that's what we do," Jill said, and Greg felt a shudder run through his body as his mom laughed an hysterical laugh. "We just die." Her shrill laughter cut at Greg's ears like a sharp knife.

Something big hit the passenger side window right next to Jill with a tremendous thud. She shrieked and threw her hands up over her face, pulling her knees up as she tried to become as small as possible. The window cracked, but held. A huge smear of blood blotted the window. "Jesus, was that a rabbit? Was that a fucking rabbit?"

Greg could hear the hysteria rising in his mom's voice. Part of him wanted to just laugh. Rabbit missiles were attacking them. That was funny. Rabbit missiles. How crazy was that? He was glad they didn't live in Australia. He could imagine what would happen if a kangaroo missile attacked them. It would probably blow up the car. He fought back a wave of giggles that desperately wanted to come out of his mouth.

"Keep it together, Jill. Keep it together."

His dad's firm voice calmed Greg. The urge to laugh went away. This wasn't funny. This wasn't funny at all. Not fucking one bit funny. He looked up at his parents, wondering if they knew he was cursing inside his head, but they were completely absorbed in the scene before them. Greg looked out the window to his right. What if it wasn't just happening here? What if it wasn't because of the thundering machine at all? What if the Earth was just fighting back after the decades of abuse it had suffered at the hands of mankind? What if it was happening all over the world?

Outside the car, the air was filled with movement.

ABOUT JACK O'DONNELL

I'm still having a lot of macabre fun exploring the Land of Fright™ and unearthing the stories I'm finding buried in those strange lands. I hope you are still having some dark fun reading them. Thanks for joining me on this second expedition into that shadowy realm of fear.

Visit www.landoffright.com and subscribe to stay up-to-date on the latest new stories in the Land of Fright™ series of horror short stories.

Or visit my author page on Amazon at www.amazon.com/author/jodonnell to see the newest releases in the Land of Fright™ series.

If you see a beam of light shining out from underneath your bed and hear strange noises, don't worry. That's probably just some denizens from the Land of Fright™ looking for a way out. Wait a minute. What the hell am I talking about? If you see a beam of light shining out from underneath your bed and hear strange noise coming from down there, get the fuck out of there. Fast.

-JACK

MORE LAND OF FRIGHT™ COLLECTIONS ARE AVAILABLE NOW!

Turn the page and step into fear!

Land of Fright™ terrorstories contained in Collection I:

#1 - Whirring Blades: A simple late-night trip to the mall for a father and his son turns into a struggle for survival when they are attacked by a deadly swarm of toy helicopters.

#2 - The Big Leagues: A scorned young baseball player shows his teammates he really knows how to play ball with the best of them.

#3 - Snowflakes: In the land of Frawst, special snowflakes are a gift from the gods, capable of transferring the knowledge of the Ancients. A young woman searches the skies with breathless anticipation for her snowflake, but finds something far more dark and dangerous instead.

#4 - End of the Rainbow: In Medieval England, a warrior and his woman find the end of a massive rainbow that has filled the sky and discover the dark secret of its power.

#5 - Trophy Wives: An enigmatic sculptor meets a beautiful woman whom he vows will be his next subject. But things may not turn out the way he plans...

#6 - Die-orama: A petty thief finds out that a WWII model diorama in his local hobby shop holds much more than just plastic vehicles and plastic soldiers.

#7 - Creature in the Creek: A lonely young woman finds her favorite secluded spot inhabited by a monster from her past.

#8 - The Emperor of Fear: In ancient Rome, two coliseum workers encounter a mysterious crate containing an unearthly creature. Just in time for the next gladiator games…

#9 - The Towers That Fell From The Sky: Two analysts race to uncover the secret purpose of the giant alien towers that have thundered down out of the skies.

#10 - God Save The Queen: An exterminator piloting an ant-sized robot comes face to face with the queen of a nest he has been assigned to destroy.

Land of Fright™ terrorstories contained in Collection III:

#21 - The Prospector: In the 1800's, a lonely prospector finds the body parts of a woman as he pans for gold in the wilds of California.

#22 - The Boy In The Yearbook: Two middle-aged women are tormented by a mysterious photograph in their high school yearbook.

#23 - Shot Glass: A man discovers the shot glasses in his great-grandfather's collection can do much more than just hold a mouthful of liquor.

#24 - The Champion: An actor in a medieval renaissance re-enactment show becomes the unbeatable champion he has longed to be.

#25 - Hitler's Graveyard: American soldiers in WWII uncover a nefarious Nazi plan to resurrect their dead heroes so they can rejoin the war.

#26 - Out of Ink: Colonists on a remote planet resort to desperate measures to ward off an attack from wild alien animals.

#27 - Dung Beetles: Mutant dung beetles attack a family on a remote Pennsylvania highway. Yes, it's as disgusting as it sounds.

#28 - The Tinies: A beleaguered office worker encounters a strange alien armada in the sub-basement of his office building.

#29 - Hammer of Charon: In ancient Rome, it is the duty of a special man to make sure gravely wounded gladiators are given a quick death after a gladiator fight. He serves his position quietly with honor. Until they try to take his hammer away from him…

#30 - Pharaoh's Cat: In ancient Egypt, the pharaoh is dying. His trusted advisors want his favorite cat to be buried with him. The cat has other plans…

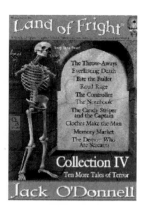

Land of Fright™ terrorstories contained in Collection IV:

Land of Fright™ terrorstories contained in Collection V:

#41 - The Hatchlings: A peaceful barbecue turns into an afternoon of terror for a suburban man when the charcoal briquets start to hatch!

#42 - Virgin Sacrifice: A professor of archaeology is determined to set the world right again using the ancient power of Aztec sacrifice rituals.

#43 - Smog Monsters: The heavily contaminated air in Beijing turns even deadlier when unearthly creatures form within the dense poison of its thick pollution.

#44 - Benders of Space-Time: A young interstellar traveler discovers the uncomfortable truth about the Benders, the creatures who power starships with their ability to fold space-time.

#45 - The Picture: A young soldier in World War II shows his fellow soldiers a picture of his beautiful fiancé during the lulls in battle. But this seemingly harmless gesture is far from innocent...

#46 - Black Ice: A vicious dragon is offered a great gift — a block of black ice to soothe the fire that burns its throat and roars in its belly. Too bad the dragon has never heard of a Trojan dwarf...

#47 - Artist Alley: At a comic book convention, a seedy comic book publisher sees himself depicted in a disturbing series of artist drawings.

#48 - Dead Zone: A yacht gets caught adrift in the dead zone in the Gulf of Mexico, trapped in an area of the sea that contains no life. What comes aboard the yacht from the depths of this dead zone in search of food cannot really be considered alive...

#49 - Cemetery Dance: A suicidal madman afraid to take his own life attempts to torment a devout Christian man into killing him.

#50 - The King Who Owned the World: A bored barbarian king demands he be brought a new challenger. But who can you find to battle a king who owns the world?

Land of Fright™ terrorstories contained in Collection VI:

#51 - Zombie Carnival: Two couples stumble upon a zombie-themed carnival and decide to join the fun.

#52 - Going Green: Drug runners trying to double cross their boss get a taste of strong voodoo magic.

#53 - Message In A Bottle: A bottle floats onto the beach of a private secluded island with an unnerving message trapped inside.

#54 - The Chase: In 18th century England, a desperate chase is on as a monstrous beast charges after a fleeing wagon, a wagon occupied by too many people...

#55 - Who's Your Daddy?: A lonely schoolteacher is disturbed by how much all of the students in her class look alike. A visit by a mysterious man sheds some light on the curious situation.

#56 - Beheaded: In 14th century England, a daughter vows revenge upon those who beheaded her father. She partners with a lascivious young warlock to restore her family's honor.

#57 - Hold Your Breath: A divorced mother of one confronts the horrible truth behind the myth of holding one's breath when driving past a cemetery.

#58 - Viral: What makes a civilization fall? Volcanoes, earthquakes, or other forces of nature? Barbarous invasions or assaults from hostile forces? Decline from within due to decadence and moral decay? Or could it be something more insidious?

#59 - Top Secret: A special forces agent confronts the villainous characters from his past, but discovers something even more dangerous. Trust.

#60 - Immortals Must Die: There is no more life force left in the universe. The attainment of immortality has depleted the world of available souls. So what do you do if you are desperate to have a child?

AND LOOK FOR EVEN MORE
LAND OF FRIGHT™ STORIES
COMING SOON!

THANKS AGAIN FOR READING.

Visit www.landoffright.com

Made in the USA
Columbia, SC
06 May 2020

96160708R00109